SNAKES
DON'T
MISS
THEIR
MOTHERS

SNAKES DON'T MISS THEIR MOTHERS

A novel by

M. E. KERR

SCHOLASTIC INC.

New York Toronto London Auckland Sydney
Mexico City New Delhi Hong Kong Buenos Aires

ISBN 0-439-77164-1

12 11 10 9 8 7 6 5 4 3 2   12 13 14 15 16/0

Printed in the U.S.A.   40

First Scholastic printing, March 2005

Typography by Amy Ryan

This book is dedicated to all the workers and volunteers at ARF, the Animal Rescue Fund of the Hamptons. And a salute to the animal shelters, all over the United States, that care for our critters, finding them good homes and loving families.

I also want to acknowledge a dedicated veterinarian, Dr. Ralph (Spike) Wester of Auburn, New York, and my friend since childhood, the late Laura Gwen Griswold Wester. They were married in the 1940s, and they lived happily together up in God's country, the Finger Lakes, until Laura Gwen's death in February 2003.

CONTENTS

The Roster at Critters
in order of appearance

MRS. SPLINTER	Director of Critters
IRVING	A twelve-year-old part-German shorthaired pointer, soap-opera devotee, and longtime Critters resident
MARSHALL	A black-and-yellow king snake who likes big words and live rats
MR. LARISSA	Faithful volunteer
PLACIDO	A one-eyed Siamese cat with a terrible secret
CATHERINE	A greyhound, rescued from the racetrack, ready to make a bet about anything
GOLDIE	A newly arrived yellow Labrador retriever, sought by Uttergore, the dogcatcher with the red gloves

DEWEY	An Irish setter who has seen better days
GINNY TINTREE	Host and volunteer to animals from Critters
FLO TINTREE	Ginny's mother, host and volunteer to animals from Critters
WALTER SPLINTER	Eleven-year-old animal lover and grandson of Critters director
NELL STAR	Host and volunteer to animals from Critters
POSH	A xoloitzcuintle, resembling a cross between a pig and a pit bull
NOEL	An iguana, left inside a Long Island Railroad train

SNAKES DON'T MISS THEIR MOTHERS

1

Is This Really Good-bye?

Irving liked to listen to the adoption interviews, even though in three years no one had ever asked to take him home.

Irving's cage was right around the corner in the kennel, but he could see the front desk at the entrance of Critters. And he could hear everything.

"Do you live in East Hampton, Mr. Twilight?"

"Yes, we live on a boat called *Summer Salt II*. Our first was lost to Hurricane Harriet down in Florida, last summer."

"How dreadful!" Mrs. Splinter eyed the tall man carefully. She was the guardian angel of the critters. She would never give an animal over to anyone she did not think was kind and responsible. "So you're new in town, Mr. Twilight?"

He had blond hair, a black crewneck sweater, and black Dockers. A big silver belt buckle. Black boots. A big smile.

"We're new for now, ma'am," he said. "We came north so my daughter could dance at Radio City Music Hall. Jimmie's in the Christmas show every year. She plays Twinkle Toes. We'll stick around to see if she gets this new job she's up for. A television commercial."

"Your daughter appears on television?" Mrs. Splinter sounded impressed, but Irving knew she probably wasn't, for her own son was a CNN newscaster.

"Jimmie hasn't been on television yet," said Mr. Twilight. "Her agent arranged an appointment for her with the head of BrainPower Limited. We've always been in show business, but we're mainly circus people."

"Oh, dear me," said Mrs. Splinter. "I don't like the way circuses treat animals. They're so often cruel."

"I wouldn't work for a circus that was cruel to its animals," Mr. Twilight said. "Where I worked, we treated all our animals like family."

"Good! But now you're leaving the circus?" Mrs. Splinter asked.

"Yes, for my daughter's sake. She needs to be with kids her own age. Regular kids. Now, with her mother gone, she needs a more normal life. I've decided to get off the road."

"What will you do, Mr. Twilight?"

"Call me Sam. I work as a clown for children's parties. And I rent the boat out for picnics and moonlight sails. This time of year, I get gigs as Santa Claus."

"And have you ever owned a cat, Sam?"

"No. My wife always had Siamese when she was a kid, but after we were married we got a little dog for Jimmie. A Boston terrier who could dance on his hind legs. I don't see any little dogs here."

"There are none," Mrs. Splinter said.

There never were little dogs in residence at Critters, not for long. Everyone wanted a cute little poodle, a terrier, a dachshund, even a bedraggled mutt, if he was small.

Irving sighed. Irving was twelve years old. He was white with great splashes of brown, and he was big. He was mostly a German shorthaired pointer, but there was a bit of English setter in him, too.

Sam Twilight said, "I couldn't bring home a dog, anyway. No dog could hold a candle to Dancer. That was our dog's name."

Mrs. Splinter said, "How old is your daughter, Mr. Twilight?"

"She's eleven, ma'am."

"I have a grandson who's that age. Walter. He's an animal lover, as I am. . . . Did you say your daughter's name was Jimmie?"

"Her name is spelled with an ie," said Sam Twilight. "My wife named her Jimmie after Jimmie Spheeris. I suppose you don't know him?"

"No, I don't."

"He was a songwriter. He was from circus people, too. So when he made it big in the Real World, my wife would make everybody listen to his songs. Then a drunk driver ran him down when he was only thirty-four. Our boat's named after one of his songs."

"Is Jimmie an animal lover?"

"Oh, yes. Her Boston terrier went to heaven at the same time her mom did, but Jimmie has carried on like the little trouper she is. That's why I want her to have a new pet to love. Pets help heal you when you're down. And when you feel up again, they're up with you! At least that's what I think."

"I think so too. Yes. Yes, Sam." Mrs. Splinter's voice was soothing, a sign she was warming to this Twilight fellow, with his sad story and his optimistic spirit. She said, "Now, you realize that the cat you picked out was declawed. His last owner had that done! He can't go outdoors. He wouldn't be able to protect himself, climb trees, scratch attackers, or any of that."

"Fine, because he'll live aboard *Summer Salt II*, which is moored at Three Mile Harbor."

"You'll have to keep him inside, you realize. If he ever fell overboard, he could not cling to anything without his claws."

"We take excellent care of animals, Mrs. Splinter. Like I said, my family considers them family."

"Well, so far so good," said Mrs. Splinter. "Do you think Jimmie would like to see Placido before you adopt him?"

"No, ma'am. It's to be a surprise."

Placido? Irving's ears pricked up, and he shook away some drool from his large lips. Don't tell me Placido's going out again, he thought. That was the way they always put it at Critters when Placido was adopted: "going out." That left room in the mind for the idea of Placido coming back. For that was what always happened when anyone took the large, one-eyed Siamese home. He went out, and then he came right back. His fake-leopard-skin carrying case was a familiar sight on the floor in the front room.

Irving doubted that Placido would last through

Christmas with the man and his daughter. It was now the twenty-third of December. Lately, Placido's usual stay was twenty-four hours.

While Mrs. Splinter explained Critters' adoption rules, Irving stood up and shook himself. The vibration was just enough to awaken Marshall, as Irving had intended. It would have done little good to bark, for Marshall had no ears. He communicated by an intricate form of reptile extrasensory perception, but he had to be awake first.

Marshall's glass cage was next to the radiator, where it was warmer. Unlike any of the other cages, his had wire mesh at the top. It was an escape-proof cage—not that Marshall had any plans to slither off to the unknown.

Marshall was the only snake at Critters.

Three feet long, black with yellow crossbands, Marshall unfurled and nosed up through the wood chips. His forked tongue darted in and out. He was cranky, Irving knew, because he had just changed his outfit. Whenever he shed his old skin, he sulked for a while and even refused to eat.

"What is going on?" he asked. He was a king who often sounded royally stern and wise. He liked big words and live rats.

"Placido's being adopted," said Irving.

"You woke me up for *that?*" Marshall was not a fan of Placido's. There was not an abundance of Placido fans at Critters, unless they were visitors who hadn't spent any time there. Placido was not easy. Word of his shenanigans' down in the cat room always reached the dogs, who thanked heaven he was a feline and not allowed in with them.

"Don't you at least want to wish Placido Merry Christmas and say good-bye?" Irving was a decent sort who forgave the faults and flaws of others.

"How many times a year am I supposed to say good-bye to Placido?" Marshall asked.

"You have a point there," said Irving. "But you've never wished him Merry Christmas."

"Placido will be back for Christmas," said Marshall, "so I'll save my breath." He relaxed into a heap by his water bowl. "My family never celebrated Christmas," he said. "We never celebrated any day. But the critters here all seem to dread Christmas. They're beginning to whine and complain more than ever."

"We get homesick this time of year," said Irving.

Marshall had arrived last Valentine's Day. The East Hampton police had brought him in. Some people had skipped out of a house without paying six months' rent, and Marshall had been found in the bathtub.

Now Mr. Larissa, the most faithful Critters volunteer worker, was heading down toward the cat room. He was carrying the empty fake-leopard case.

News of the adoption began to spread among the dogs.

Mr. Larissa went into the cat room, swinging the doors open with a joyful motion, pleased that a cat would get a home for the holidays. The dogs caught a brief glimpse of the felines lolling about on the thick green rug, crawling around the carpeted shelves, pawing at leftover summer flies groggily climbing up the windows.

"Wake up, Placido!" Mr. Larissa sang out. "You have a new home!"

The door closed before a sneaky calico cat could make a break for the hall.

"I never had any home but the racetrack," said a very skinny greyhound wistfully. "But I'll make a bet that Placido will be back before our Christmas stockings are put out. Who wants to bet?" Catherine had been in many dog-track races, and she had acquired a fondness for gambling. She often took bets on things that were happening at Critters.

"*I'll* bet," said a yellow Labrador retriever, who did not really know the Siamese cat. He had arrived only a week ago, no dog tags on him. He had jumped out the window of his family's car when his sharp eye had spotted a rabbit off in the fields. Then he had run loose for days and miles, lost and scared. His family had just moved to Long Island, and the land was strange to him. Although he did not appreciate it at the moment, he was a lucky dog. If the dogcatcher had found him, he would have been spending Christmas in a dark, damp basement with arachnids and rats.

His real name was Rex, but at Critters they'd named him Goldie.

"Goldie? I'll bet you my Christmas stocking that Placido will be returned in a day!" said Catherine.

"That's a bet!" Goldie said. "Even if he doesn't work out, I bet people would let him stay for Christmas."

"Any other takers?" Catherine called out.

No one spoke up.

Then Mr. Larissa reappeared. This time his right shoulder was tilted from the weight of the fourteen-pound Siamese cat inside the carrier.

"Wish Placido a Merry Christmas, everyone!" he said.

"Merry Christmas," said everyone but Marshall, who would wait until Placido returned.

Mr. Larissa stopped by the cages for a moment and

said, "Oh, I know you all feel lonely because it's Christmastime. But don't give up hope. One day you'll be adopted too!"

Irving's tail barely thumped as Placido passed by. Irving wasn't in a joyful mood. It would be his third Christmas at Critters. It was not that bad a place, but it was not a real home. Still, it was warm and the food was good. There were the Christmas stockings, too, each one containing a ball and two lamb-and-rice sticks, which were Catherine's favorite treat.

"Good-bye, everyone!" Placido's nose was pressed against the airholes. "Good-bye!"

Once again, the creatures at Critters called out hopefully, "Good-bye, Placido!"

"Good riddance," some of them said under their breaths, particularly the felines, for they were the ones at his mercy when he was in residence.

2

A Special Child

He was a special child with the face of a Botticelli angel and the disposition of a little lamb. Oh, he was special, was this little baby, and he was given a very special name: Percival Kermit Uttergore. When he was old enough to give orders, somewhere between ages three and five, he had his parents strike the name Kermit from all the records, since there was a frog by that name on national television.

He was not going to bear a frog's name, not this special, golden-haired, blue-eyed boy everyone said was a genius and might one day even be a corporate head or a talk-show host.

He had not, sad to say, grown up to be a corporate head nor a talk-show host, but he did have one of those license plates with just two initials, and there was a rather remarkable logo, painted by his own hand, on each side of his old, rusting brown Bronco.

P U, his license plates read.

A pair of gloves, the color of cherries, adorned each door.

"What's *that?*" he shouted into his cell phone, slowing up to hear better. "What's *that?*" he repeated. He blamed his deafness on the barking dogs he fetched from garbage dumps, storefronts, alleys, and pastures: wretches that were lost or unwanted.

When there was a reward for the dog, he sent his ailing sister to collect it. As a salaried public servant he was not allowed to take a reward for what he was paid to do.

His ailing sister was given one percent for herself. Percival Uttergore gave it grudgingly, but it was proof, nonetheless, of the old adage that no one is *all* bad.

His ailing sister had telephoned Uttergore in his van to alert him that there were new lost-dog posters everywhere—on telephone poles, in store windows, on supermarket bulletin boards, fastened under the windshield wipers of parked cars—you name it and a poster was sure to be there. So said Ursula Uttergore.

"What kind of dog?" he demanded. "Speak up, Ursula!"

"Please" and "thank you" had been dropped from his vocabulary soon after Kermit had been eliminated from his name.

His once-curly blond hair was now brown and filled with soot, dandruff, and yellow scales that perhaps would wash out in a shampoo, though that had not been tried for a long time.

The baby-blue eyes were bloodshot, and he had a beard to protect his face from shaving.

Filthy was he, and he reeked so badly that his wife had run off, taking with her Percival Uttergore Junior, a bully who hung out at bowling alleys reading comic books.

But year after year Mr. Uttergore was reelected dogcatcher, for no one else ever ran for that office.

"I don't give a *whistle* that his name is Rex! What kind of dog is he?"

His ailing sister replied that it was a yellow Labrador retriever.

Some dogs that came into his cellar he sold to laboratories doing research, particularly dogs that were healthy, that had not been lost for very long. This retriever sounded like just such a dog.

Uttergore got out his red wool gloves and stepped on the gas.

3

Ahoy!

Before his lovely blue right eye was punctured beyond repair, Placido had won so many ribbons at cat shows, he could not count them all on four paws. He had been the only cat at the breeder's who was free to stroll from the cattery to the house, where he would climb to the back of the couch to be admired. He was a purebred seal-point Siamese, once known as Prince from Siam. He had had a sterling silver bowl with his name on it. He had had a sterling silver mirror and comb. He had had his own scrapbook. In those days he had had his way. He had kneaded Persian rugs and clawed the arms of hand-embroidered Regency sofas. No one dared spank him, for he was a prize winner, temperamental by nature.

Look what he had come to! Look how far he had fallen!

A boat! They expected him to live on a boat!

Last night the man had opened a can of smelly fish and put it on top of a newspaper, on the galley table. Then he had put Placido on the table, too, and said, "I have a date to play Santa Claus at the mall, Placido. This is din din, buddy boy! Eat it all up! It's mackerel!"

Placido had had all he could do to keep from gobbling it down. But he had decided not to. A good thing to do was take a whiff, then use his front paws to make the motions, back and forth around the cat dish, of covering up some foul thing. Just as though he had been served roadkill.

A good mood to be in on a boat was a bad mood.

The thing about the girl was that when she decided to listen to music, she listened to the same songs over and over. Last night it was "Sighs in a Shell," "Sunken Skies," and "The Dragon Is Dancing." Over and over.

This morning the girl watched the same tape. Over and over.

There she was dancing with the bulbous-eyed Boston terrier. How many times was Placido to be subjected to that vile Christmas song?

Nobody knows
But Twinkle Toes
What fun it is to dance!
Her doggie knows—
Yes, Dancer knows,
For see him up on his doggie toes!
But no human soul,
Nor the sole on a shoe,
Will ever dance the way you do.
Twinkle Toes!
Twinkle Toes!
Dance while it snows!
Twinkle Toes!

He had to watch the girl and the wretched Boston terrier dance about in a fake snowstorm on a large stage.

The girl was going to New York shortly, minus the dog, for the pitifully unattractive Boston terrier had gone to bye-bye land forever.

"Placido?" the girl called out. "Placido, I have a one-o'clock appointment and a two-o'clock curtain! I am *leaving*! Wherever you are, good-bye, Placido!"

A good place to hide was up in the master's cabin behind a bunk. There he could see everything without being seen.

On the tape the girl was introduced as Twinkle Toes, "with her precious pet, Dancer." But her real name was Jimmie, the name her father called her. Her father had left early that morning, dressed again as Santa Claus, heading for a nearby mall.

Both the girl and the father talked to themselves when they were alone, which they seemed to think they were even though Placido was there. Not by any choice of his own.

Jimmie would say things like "Working on Christmas Day sucks."

Sam Twilight would ask her not to say "sucks." It made her sound too tough.

Placido would never have chosen to live with performers. He had had enough of that at Madame de Flute's.

He had learned there that performers were even more self-involved than parrots, who were known to be content in a cage with nothing but a mirror to entertain them.

Performers were basket cases right before auditions, and thus Placido was on a boat with a basket case who had an appointment before her show with Quintin Quick, the C.E.O. of BrainPower Limited.

"PLA-CI-DO!"

It was a desperate sound like a coyote howling in the moonlight, but it would get her nowhere. She had a lot to learn about the feline disposition, quite different from the sickening, desperate-for-attention canine personality.

Then there came a knock on the door.

"This could be my limousine, Placido! If this is StarStretch, I have to leave immediately!"

Leave! Placido shrugged. Don't worry about a new cat in strange surroundings!

Knock, knock again.

"Hello? Who is it?" Jimmie called out.

Her long blond hair bounced as she walked from the galley through the cabin to the door. She was in her street clothes, of course. Only a nonprofessional ever walked around in costume in public. Placido had learned that from Madame de Flute. He had learned quite a lot from Madame until a certain parrot had entered their lives and ruined everything.

Jimmie had on a pink miniskirt over black leggings, with a black sweater that had been her mother's.

Mr. Twilight had asked her how long she planned to wear clothes that were too big for her, and she had answered, "When you stop humming 'Eternity Spin,'

I'll give away her things."

"Touché," he said, which was a French word meaning whatever it was you said was to the point. Sometimes fencers used it when an opponent's foil nicked them. That was the trouble with human language. There were many words for one thing, and the same word for many things. Why? Placido had no idea why. It was the way things were in this cock-eyed world, which was both cruel and kind, so never mind those who tell you that you cannot have it both ways.

When the girl opened the door, who stood there but Mr. Larissa and Mrs. Splinter's grandson, Walter. Ye gods and little fishes! Had they come for Placido?

Placido fled to an upper bunk.

"Are you Mr. Twilight's daughter?" asked Mr. Larissa.

"Maximum, five minutes. I have a show to do, babes," said Jimmie, slipping into the jaded jargon of the fast-living stars of stage and screen. "What are you selling?"

"I'm Mr. Larissa," the man said, "and this is Walter Splinter. We're from Critters. How is Placido doing?"

"He just got here yesterday," said Jimmie.

"I know. But we'll be closed tomorrow, Christmas

Day. We like to be sure the adoption is working, that both you and Placido are satisfied."

"We're doing okay, I guess," said Jimmie.

"It is better for both you and the animal, if there is anything wrong, to nullify the adoption."

"We always check right away," said Walter. "Some people will just put the animal out the door if it doesn't look like it's working. That's how Percival Uttergore gets most of his."

"Who's Percival Uttergore?"

"The dogcatcher," said Walter. "He wears red gloves."

"There's a snowstorm predicted," said Mr. Larissa, "and it's getting colder. We brought your mail in so it won't get wet."

"Placido was once a very famous cat," said Walter. "He was a star who won many prizes."

"How did he come by that tacky faux-leopard carrying case?" said Jimmie. "I can't bear to see him plopped back in that thing and toted off to Critters."

"Is Placido eating?" said Walter. "Is he purring?"

The man said, "Walter always worries when a new pet is adopted, particularly when it's a surprise for someone. We call him the Worry Wart."

"How *are* you two getting along together?" Walter asked.

"It's hard to say."

"But do you like him?" Walter persisted.

The girl shrugged. "Sure," she said. "Sure."

Then Jimmie saw the very long StarStretch limo pulling up at the dock. You could hear its expensive motor running.

"There's my ride," she said. "I have to rush. Come back another time."

"I'll leave your mail here on the table!" said Mr. Larissa.

Saved by the Bentley, Placido said to himself as he eyed the elegant motorcar and remembered better days, when he rode behind a chauffeur and received catnip balls from the cashier at the drive-in window of the Morgan Trust bank.

4
Exmus Card

Durest Jimmie and Sam,

Last night we hunk aroun the pie car n someone playd an old cd of Jimmie Spheeris so we thoghtof you guys and also of poor Elaine, n Dancer. Merry Christmas anyways from Check.

P.S. Shirley learning trapese. She sez hi n remine Jimmie in the Real World don't call people lot lice, rubes, townies or it giveaway your from circus. Movie stars an others call them civilians. Shirley knows you want to suckseed someplace els. She sez have a good exmus.

5
An Average Child

He was an average child with a face no one ever seemed able to remember, including his parents, who called him Quintin, for he was their fifth boy. That made him easy to spot among the others, as he was shorter and in a lower grade than they were, and if he spoke he was easily identifiable, for he lisped and stuttered. He much preferred listening. He listened to the radio, books on tape, teachers, and his older brothers.

His parents were disappointed when he brought home his failing report cards with the only As in manageability, but that was one less son to send to college, saving them thousands and thousands of dollars.

While his brothers became lawyers and doctors

and talk-show hosts, he would undoubtedly have a less glitzy career. He could sell things behind a counter or become a dogcatcher. The Smiths' other boys would bring them honors. This fifth one was a maverick, a word Quintin Smith had heard on the radio and believed described him: a person with unorthodox ideas.

"Whatever you say," said his parents, who had no clue what his ideas were, since he seldom spoke.

After high school he invented a word game that brought him some earnings—until his idea was stolen by Barker Brothers, and he was left to his own devices again.

The ordinary name Smith bothered him, even though he did not love his parents any less. He changed his name to Quintin Quick, simply because the clerk at the change-of-name bureau grew impatient with his stuttering and stammering and shouted out, "Patience is not my forte! Quick!"

That was how Quintin Smith became Quintin Quick, soon to be a corporate head.

But not before he touched the impatient clerk's sleeve and said, "Excuth me? You just pronounced forte fortay. Tch! Tch! It's never pronounced that way except by musicians and f-f-f-fools. You must say fort. People will think the b-b-b-better of you for it."

For Quintin Quick's forte (rhymes with sort), after years of listening, had become words. They would make both his lisp and his stutter disappear eventually. They would make him rich, and they would make him obnoxious.

6

Consensus of Opinion

"'m Mr. Quick, the C.E.O. of BrainPower Limited. Do you remember me? We met in Miami last summer, after your show. You've grown taller."

"Not much taller," said Jimmie Twilight.

"Not an inch taller," said Ms. Fondaloot, a casting agent of importance. "She's the same height exactly!" Ms. Fondaloot paced around the studio in her high-heeled boots, wearing her rose-tinted shades.

"You see, I'm looking for someone who'll look like a teenager."

"I believe you're right: She *has* grown taller," said Ms. Fondaloot, "and she'll shoot up some more, too."

"She *seems* taller," said an assistant to Mr. Quick,

who was eager to wind up this casting call and have Christmas Eve with his family.

The girl spoke up again. "The consensus of opinion seems to be that I *have* grown taller."

"Do you realize what you just said?" Mr. Quick asked the girl.

"I said I guess I have grown taller."

"That isn't what you said," said Mr. Quick. "What you said was the general agreement of opinion of opinion."

"I didn't say that!" the girl said.

"I didn't hear her say that!" said Ms. Fondaloot.

"Consensus means a general agreement of opinion. When you say 'consensus of opinion' you're saying the 'general agreement of opinion of opinion.' It's redundant . . . and worse, it's not smart. I'm looking for someone who'll appear to be very smart."

"She's very, very smart," said Ms. Fondaloot.

"Thank you for coming in on the day before Christmas," said Mr. Quick.

"No problem," said Ms. Fondaloot. "Jimmie works at Radio City Music Hall every year in the Christmas show. She's Twinkle Toes."

"If you get this job," Mr. Quick said, "you'll be called Jane Brain. You'll be the spokesgirl for our hot new learning game, Brainstorm. Jane

Brainstorms French. Jane Brainstorms history. That sort of thing . . . Do you still have that smart little dancing dog?"

"Not anymore," said the girl.

"Of course, if you want a dancing dog with her, that's easy to arrange," said Ms. Fondaloot. "I have animal clients, too."

Mr. Quick waved away the suggestion. "No, no, you couldn't find a dog as smart as that one. He was a pro!"

"I happen to have a pood—"

Mr. Quick didn't let Ms. Fondaloot continue. "Good luck, young lady. I'll be back in the booth watching."

After the assistant led the girl to a small stage, she was handed a sheet with her dialogue underlined in blue pencil.

Waiting there was a boy called Art Smart, with his own sheet of dialogue.

"Ready?" a woman shouted from the shadows.

"Ready!" the boy shouted back.

"Go!"

GIRL: I'm Jane. I wasn't always a brain.

BOY: I remember. You thought Cuba was in Brazil.

GIRL: Now I know that Cuba is in the Caribbean Sea and its capital is Havana; population, eleven million; currency, peso; area, forty-three thousand square miles.

BOY: Excuse me, Jane, but have you been Brainstorming geography?

GIRL: Geography, history, French, Spanish. Name any subject, Art Smart, and I bet I've Brainstormed it.

BOY: How about Buddhism, Jane?

GIRL: A yogin is one who practices mental training or discipline. *Eh ma!* is a Tibetan exclamation of astonishment or wonder.

BOY: *Eh ma*, Jane. I'm impressed.

GIRL: In one short month I have managed to impress Art Smart. You can impress people too. You can buy the Brainstorm books, or learn from the Brainstorm tapes. However you choose to do it, you're going to like yourself.

BOY: You're going to *like* being a brain.

Ms. Fondaloot was waiting by the door, holding Jimmie's coat for her, telling her not to bother with her boots, there wasn't time.

"We have a car waiting," she said. "We'll just make it to Radio City."

Inside the car there was silence for some seconds, and then Ms. Fondaloot sucked her breath in with a slight *sssss* sound, signaling that she was fighting to control her appalling temper.

Her voice was low and restrained as she said, "I *wish* you hadn't spoken out of turn. I *wish* you hadn't said 'consensus of opinion.'"

7

"What Do You Bet?"

"It's five o'clock Christmas Eve," said Goldie triumphantly. "We're closed for the holiday now, and there's no sign of Placido!"

"There's no sign of our Christmas stockings either," said Catherine. "I have my heart set on those lamb-and-rice sticks. Yum, yum."

Irving said, "They're coming. I can see Mrs. Splinter out at the desk sorting them."

"Just a minute, Catherine," said Goldie. "Remember our bet. I get mine and yours, too."

"It's only Christmas Eve. You don't get my stocking until the stroke of midnight on Christmas. Placido will surely be back by then."

"You are a sore loser, Catherine," said Goldie. "I

heard that no one comes here on Christmas Day but Walter and the volunteer walkers. So far Placido has made it! He has a home, at least he does for Christmas."

"The man who took him will probably leave him at the door in that tawdry carrying case. Critters doesn't have to be open to have Placido returned. Desperate people come up with desperate solutions."

Irving gave a sharp bark. "Be fair, Catherine!"

"Why should *I* be fair?" Catherine said. "Don't talk to me about fair. Was it fair that I was dumped here after I won every race for two years?"

"Just be glad that Mrs. Splinter took you in," said Irving. "Most used-up greyhounds go to heaven when their racing days are over."

"Who are you calling used up?" Catherine demanded.

Then Marshall slid up the side of his glass case, his tongue darting in and out. "*Life* isn't fair," he said. "Those policemen who found me in the bathtub tossed me into a wicker clothes hamper as though I were soiled laundry. That's how *I*, a *king*, ended up here surrounded by such depauperate strays!"

"'Depauperate'?" Catherine said. "What does that word mean?"

"It means 'stunted, severely diminished, arrested in development.' Look around you, my dear lady," the snake replied.

"I," said Goldie, rising up on all fours, "am a yellow Labrador retriever! When my master's father took me hunting, I went into the icy bay to bring back the ducks. I am known for my ability to swim! And here I am in a kennel for the homeless, including a serpent!"

Irving chuckled at the idea of Goldie hunting. He knew from experience quite a lot about hunting, although he disliked swimming and water.

"Some hunter you must have been, Goldie," he teased. "You can't even point."

"That's right," Marshall chimed in. "At least Irving can point."

"Not like a setter, though." Dewey finally spoke up, although he rarely got involved in these silly arguments. But his Irish was up, for he was a purebred Irish setter, a red-coated trained bird dog. Yes, he was old. He had outlived his master, which was how he had come to Critters; how Irving had come to Critters, too. But everyone knew the Irish setter was the most handsome, most skilled of all the pointing breeds.

Goldie said, "I was never reduced to pointing. I

went right in and retrieved the game."

Dewey said, "Ask any duck shooter whether he'd rather hunt with a retriever or a setter. Catherine? Do you want to bet? The answer is a setter!"

Now Irving was up on all fours, too, barking his irritation at both Goldie and Dewey. And down the line a water spaniel was beginning to boast about his hunting and swimming abilities. In the next cage a foxhound was remembering the chase.

Then Mrs. Splinter's voice rang out. "Merry, Merry, Merry Christmas, everyone!" She was a tiny, white-haired woman who wore a white stocking cap with a red tassel and a white ball. "Mrs. Santa Splinter is here with your stockings!"

"Two for me!" Goldie looked across at Catherine. "And none for you!"

It is just a good thing humans cannot understand animal talk.

But never mind the mean-spirited things Goldie and Catherine were shouting at each other; Mrs. Splinter was in a festive mood. "Does everyone have the Christmas spirit?" she said. "It's starting to snow out! We're going to have a white Christmas!"

Then the dogs forgot their arguments and all began to bark gaily.

All but Catherine, who was never warm, and who

also always shivered when she feared she had lost a bet.

Mrs. Splinter paused by Catherine's cage. She looped Catherine's leash around the handle. "Are you sad, darling? Don't be," she said. "Ginny Tintree has invited you to her home for all of Christmas weekend, starting tonight. Every year she takes a dog for the holidays. I wish all our volunteers were that generous."

Marshall said, "Why just for the holidays, if she's so generous?"

"Because the Star-Tintrees already have a dog, and a daughter, plus they run the tree farm," said Irving. "I was there two Christmases ago."

"What are they like?" Catherine asked, dancing about with excitement.

"Little Sun Lily can speak Chinese because she happens to be Chinese. Nell Star is a news freak and a landscaper. Ginny Tintree is the brains behind the business. She handles the money."

Marshall began to giggle meanly. "Don't forget the chanteuse who comes to visit with them on holidays. Placido told me all about her."

"It's just Ginny's mother, Mrs. Tintree," said Irving. "Her first name is Flo, and she's an animal lover just like Mrs. Splinter."

"And Walter, and Mr. Larissa, and on and on,"

said Marshall. "We attract zoophiles here at Critters."

"Attract what?" Catherine asked.

"A zoophile is simply someone who has a fondness for animals," said Marshall. "I need a nap, I think. I'm so very hungry I'm lethargic. I wish Mrs. Splinter would serve our Christmas snacks."

Instead of a stocking with chew sticks and dog biscuits, for Christmas Marshall always received a defrosted mouse, which was in a Baggie on the office desk.

"Guess what!" Mrs. Splinter said. "The Star-Tintrees had a party today."

It was her custom to babble away as she went among the animals. But the Star-Tintrees' having a party was *hardly* a guess what, Irving thought. That family was always having parties. When Irving was their Christmas dog, they had a party for fifteen—five kids from the Ross School and their parents.

Once, for a party, Mrs. Tintree had borrowed Placido. As she began to sing "Soft I Am and Purr I Do," Placido had jumped from her lap, run behind Ginny and Nell's expensive printed linen drapes, and tangled himself up in them until he brought them down with a crash.

He had been returned to Critters in disgrace,

marching angrily about the cat room, his tail whipping in the air, his dignity outraged.

Mrs. Splinter continued talking to the animals waiting for their Christmas stockings. "Guess what! The Star-Tintrees hired Placido's new owner to play Santa Claus! He might still be there, Catherine. You might meet him and learn how Placido is doing. Ginny Tintree left the party just to come here for you."

Never one to lose her gambling spirit, even in blissful moments, Catherine sat on her haunches and said, "Who wants to bet that when I come back from the Star-Tintrees' in three days, Placido will be here?"

"You have nothing left to bet," said Irving.

"Just bet," said Catherine. "We don't have to bet anything."

"No one wants to bet just to bet," said Irving. "Relax, Catherine, if you know how."

Everyone joined in as Mrs. Splinter came back to take Catherine away on her leash. "Merry Christmas, Catherine! We'll miss you!"

"Merry Christmas!" Catherine answered, even though she had no idea what it really meant, or what people did on Christmas. She had spent most of her life at a track kennel in a stacked cage. She had been let loose only four times a day in a small turnout pen, to do number one and number two.

Marshall dangled woefully from a branch of the plastic palm tree a volunteer had contributed to his cage. Then he slumped to the wood chips and curled into a tight, depressed circle. Mrs. Splinter, in her excitement over Catherine's invitation to the Star-Tintrees', had forgotten to give Marshall his Christmas mouse.

8

SUN LILY

Catherine rode in the back of the black Land Rover, her thin tail spanking the tan leather seat with excitement. Since the Star-Tintree farm was a tree farm, out in front there was a string of lights, with some last-minute shoppers buying Christmas trees. Catherine was becoming more and more excited. At the racetrack the greyhounds did not celebrate Christmas, even though there were decorative wreaths on the stall doors.

The Land Rover went up a long driveway in the snow and stopped in front of a redbrick house.

A small child began to jump up and down on the sidewalk.

"Sun Lily is here to greet you, Catherine," said Ginny Tintree.

The little girl with black hair and almond-shaped eyes was grinning. She had on a red sweater, red ear-muffs, and black riding pants with black boots.

Ginny opened the car door and cried out, "Sun Lily, Mummy has brought home your Christmas dog!"

"He's a whippet!" Sun Lily said, dancing up and down.

"No, sweetheart, it's a she and she's a greyhound. Catherine is one of the racetrack dogs Mrs. Splinter saved from being put to sleep."

"Or being taken away by Percival Uttergore. Or being sold to a university hospital for experiments. That's what Nell said."

"Nell is right, I'm sorry to say." Ginny Tintree had long blond hair, and she was smiling at Catherine as she waited patiently for the greyhound to step out of the car.

"She's so scared, isn't she, Mummy?" Sun Lily reached out to pet Catherine, who flinched, not meaning to but not used to someone so small touching her.

"Don't be scared, Catherine," Sun Lily said. "No one will harm you here."

"Remember, Sun Lily," said Ginny, "she's not used to a child, nor a house."

"What about when she sees Peke?"

"She's been living in a kennel full of dogs, so Peke probably won't surprise her. We'll introduce them gradually."

They began walking toward the house.

"How can people be so cruel to greyhounds and horses?" Sun Lily asked.

Ginny Tintree said, "A lot of the owners of racing dogs and also racing horses don't think of them as pets. They're simply investments. When their racing days are over, they are of no use, and their racing days don't last that long."

"I love Mrs. Splinter for taking Catherine in!" said Sun Lily. "And I love you, Catherine!"

"*Woof! Woof!*" Catherine decided that the feeling suddenly overwhelming her was happiness. She had never had such a delicious feeling before.

Inside the large redbrick house there was an enormous Christmas tree in the hall. It had blinking blue lights, blue and silver ornaments, and silver tinsel. Underneath there were many wrapped packages.

"Hello, Catherine," said Nell. "Remember me? I took you out a few times." She gave Catherine a friendly pat on the head.

Catherine certainly did remember her. Nell had hair as black as Sun Lily's, and she was tall and husky.

You didn't go on walks with Nell. You went on runs. Nell was the volunteer who usually asked for Goldie, too, and tried to run with him. Goldie told the critters he always felt sorry for giving Nell such a hard time, but he could not help himself. He dreamed of getting free to search for Bob, the boy who owned him, so Goldie pulled hard on the leash and kept barking. But Nell was patient, Goldie always told the others. Nell was his favorite volunteer.

"Our party is over already," said Sun Lily, "or we could have given you some cake and ice cream, Catherine."

Catherine wondered what cake tasted like. She doubted she'd like anything with ice in it, since her teeth and gums were in bad shape. Even falling snow hurt them.

"We let Santa Claus go home early, Ginny," Nell Star said. "After all, it *is* Christmas Eve, and Sam Twilight has a daughter to be with."

"We're having another party soon," Ginny Tintree said.

"On New Year's Eve," Nell said, "and we've already asked Mr. Twilight to entertain."

"How about a party on Chinese New Year?" Sun Lily said.

"Why not?" Nell laughed.

* * *

Catherine heard some dog yips coming from another room in the house. She looked up at Ginny and Nell with concerned eyes.

Nell said, "That's right, Catherine, there's another dog here. You're going to meet him later. Right now we want you to get used to the downstairs."

"Let's show Catherine her bed and her dinner bowl!" Sun Lily said.

"Not now, sweetheart," said Ginny Tintree. "The news is coming on. You know how Nell feels about the nightly news."

"Why do *we* have to watch it?" said Sun Lily. "We don't feel that way."

"I do," said Ginny. "I like to know what's going on in the world."

Catherine followed along as they all went into the living room, where the television was.

"Nell? When shall we tell Mummy what Santa Claus told us about the boy at the mall?" Sun Lily asked.

"Can we wait until after the news?" Nell asked.

"Let's compromise," Ginny said. "Let's wait until the first commercial."

The three of them sat on the long blue-velvet sofa facing the TV.

Catherine sat beside the sofa. She had heard television before from the office at Critters, where

Mrs. Splinter watched soaps. But only Irving could see it from his cage. He was particularly fond of *Days of Our Lives*. No one dared whimper or bark when *Days of Our Lives* was on.

"Good evening," said the man on TV. "This is Guy Splinter reporting from Israel."

"So that's where he is now," said Ginny.

"Israel is only about the size of New Jersey," said Sun Lily. "We learned that in school."

"Good for you, honey!" Ginny said.

"New Jersey is where Guy Splinter's ex-wife lives now," said Sun Lily. "She's Walter's mother!"

"The town crier knows all the gossip, don't you, Sun Lily?" Nell chuckled.

"I know Guy Splinter is Mrs. Splinter's son!" Sun Lily said. "And I know that he's Walter Splinter's father. Another thing I know is Santa's real name. It's—"

"Put a lid on it, Gossip Gertie," Nell said. "I want to hear the news."

When the commercials came on, Sun Lily said, "Mummy, is Santa Claus' real name Mr. Twilight?"

"He's one of Santa's helpers who dresses up like Santa," said Nell.

"Mummy, when I told him you were bringing

Catherine from Critters, he said he just adopted a cat named Placido from Critters."

"So that's who has Placido," Ginny said.

"But that's not all, Mummy! Mr. Twilight was playing Santa Claus at the Riverhead Mall this morning. There was a young boy there with his little sister. She told Santa Claus what she wanted for Christmas was for her brother to get his dog back. He lost his dog, and it's a yellow Labrador retriever!"

Nell said, "The family just moved to Long Island. The boy loosened his dog's collar during a drive. The dog saw a rabbit and jumped right out the car window."

I would have done the same thing, Catherine thought. I would have jumped off a train or jumped out of a plane for a rabbit.

"It couldn't be Goldie's owner, could it?" Ginny asked.

"It's such a long shot," Nell told Ginny. "I'm not letting myself get excited yet."

"The boy's name is Bob," Sun Lily said.

Bob. Catherine's ears twitched.

"They're from Montauk, Mummy! But because they're new, they never heard of Critters."

Nell Star said, "I don't dare hope."

Dare, Catherine would have said if she could talk

people's language. Dare, because Goldie's owner is named Bob.

"Just on the chance the dog could be at Critters, Mr. Twilight wrote down the address and gave it to Bob's mother," said Nell.

"Oh, I pray it's Goldie!" said Ginny.

"He said his dog's name is Rex," Sun Lily said. "You can see if he answers to that name!"

"Good idea, Sun Lily!"

"Quiet, please," said Nell. "The news is back on."

Catherine breathed a sigh of contentment and lay down on the soft living-room rug. The only other rug she had ever been on was in Mrs. Splinter's office at Critters, but it was not a thick rug like this one. There was a rug in the cat room, too, but the dogs could not have rugs in their cages because some dogs were not housebroken. There was no way to hose down the kennels mornings with wet rugs inside the cages. Unlike cats, dogs were not going to use kitty litter.

Catherine put all those practical considerations out of her mind and concentrated on the idea that Goldie was this Bob's lost dog. Catherine was sure of it, for Goldie had told everyone his real name was Rex.

Even though right at that very moment Goldie was probably eating the lamb-and-rice sticks he had won from Catherine, Catherine would not hold it against him. Catherine was known to be something of a sore loser, but she was happy for the first time ever in her life. There were not that many happy gamblers in the world either.

The yipping from the upstairs in the house became wailing, barking, whining, until Nell slapped her hand on her knee and said, "Damn Peke!"

"Damn Peke!" said Sun Lily. "We can't hear the news!"

"Don't *you* get surly," Ginny told her. "One surly person in this family is enough!"

Soon after Ginny had spoken, from the corner of her eye, Catherine caught sight of a small dog who had suddenly appeared by the Christmas tree in the hall. Catherine stood and immediately went to attention, body rigid, ears up, tail up.

What was the little beast doing? There was a white ribbon in his mouth, and he was tugging at it. It was tied around a large red package, and Catherine saw that now this peculiar creature was running off with the ribbon.

Catherine began to bark, great loud barks of alarm!

Barks that said, "Thief! Ribbon thief!"

Barks that even brought Nell to her feet to shout, "Peke! You're going to get it, Peke! What have you done?"

9

A Warning from a Snake

One thing Irving did not need was to see a snake swallow a mouse whole on Christmas Eve.

He turned his face away and put his nose down between his paws.

"My grandmother forgot all about you, didn't she, Marshall?" said Walter Splinter as he dropped the dead rodent into Marshall's cage. "I was worried that she wouldn't remember, so I sneaked over to give it to you."

The dogs never barked those evenings Walter paid surprise visits. They all understood he'd get in trouble if Mrs. Splinter found out he was there. It was against her rules for him to enter Critters alone, at night. But he was often worried about one thing or another, and he would sneak in to see that everything was all right.

The dogs raised their heads when the lights went on, but they knew his step by now and fell back asleep.

His blond hair was covered with snow. So was the leather jacket his father had sent him from Italy last year.

It must be coming down very hard outside, Irving mused. That meant the volunteers wouldn't be able to take out the dogs on their morning walks. Christmas Day all the dogs would be grumpy and sorry for themselves. The cats would be chasing their tails, drunk on Christmas catnip.

"I guess everyone's asleep," said Walter. "Grandma fell asleep right after dinner. But I'm waiting for my mother to come."

Irving shook himself so Walter would know not *everyone* was asleep. Not everyone could sleep through the sounds of Marshall's thrashing about, hitting the sides of his cage, as the mouse disappeared inside him.

Marshall had not had a good meal for a long time, so the mouse was a welcome treat.

The clock on the wall said ten thirty.

If Catherine had been there, she would be waking

51

the others to take bets that Walter's mother wouldn't show up. Goldie would be the only dog to bet she would, since everyone else at Critters knew Walter's mother all too well.

It was Marshall who knew the most about Walter's family. Walter was one of the rare humans who ever paid attention to the snake. Often when the dogs were being walked by the volunteers, Walter kept Marshall company. That was when he confided in Marshall.

By the time the dogs came back panting and thirsty, Marshall would know where Guy Splinter's next assignment would take him.

Marshall would also know how the mother was doing, off in New Jersey with Walter's stepfather and his four little stepsisters.

"So you're awake, Irving," said Walter. "And you've eaten everything in your stocking. We had turkey. I can't bring you turkey bones, because they are bad for you; pieces of bone could get stuck in your throat. But I'll bring you a slice tomorrow. Grandma and I had a whole turkey to ourselves. At nine o'clock we decided not to wait any longer for my mother."

A wise decision, from Irving's point of view.

Irving had seen Olivia Splinter only once. She

was a pretty thing for a human female, but she was always in a hurry. She was always saying things like "I would love to see the new Dalmatian, Walter, but there isn't time!" She would say, "I'm on a tight schedule," and "Next time I'll spend the whole afternoon with you!"

Irving was standing so Walter could tickle him behind his ears. Ecstasy. Irving closed his eyes, only to open them and see the bulge in Marshall's body. Now came the job of choking it down to where he could digest it.

Snakes were really gross!

As much as Irving liked Marshall, who always took his side in arguments, he had to admit that his table manners were revolting!

Even Goldie awakened, shook his head so hard his Critters tags rattled, and said, "That snake makes me sick! How can you stand to be next to him, Irving?"

"Marshall can't help what he is," said Irving philosophically. "We are what we are, even when we are snakes."

Walter moved down to Goldie's cage. "How're you doing, fellow?" he said. "Are you a lonesome boy tonight?"

Goldie let out a little yelp, and Walter reached in and petted him. "It's hard to be away from your family on Christmas. My dad's in Israel, but my mother's on her way here."

In your dreams, Irving said to himself.

Outside, the wind was whistling.

"No one is going to plow out this place on Christmas Day!" Irving said to Goldie. "We won't get our walks."

The bulge in Marshall's body was growing larger.

"One thing I'd never eat is a rodent," said Irving.

"Lotho blatho," Marshall answered.

"Don't talk with your sides full, please," said Irving.

"I thought he didn't talk when he ate," Goldie said.

"He almost never does," Irving said.

Walter had shut Goldie's cage and dimmed the lights.

"I think I'll check out the cat room," he said. "They must miss Placido."

Not, Irving and Goldie agreed.

All the creatures at Critters knew how Placido had controlled the cat room. He had a bad reputation. He would wait until the cats were settled in their sun spots mornings, and then one after the other he would nudge them out of their places, as though the sun were solely his property.

At night Placido had roamed through the room with his tail switching, seeing which cat was sleeping the soundest. Then he would pounce.

He always dove into the feeding tray before the others got there, licking off all the broth, gobbling up the choice pieces . . . and never mind what followed one of his feeding frenzies. You could hear the *urps* all the way to Mrs. Splinter's office.

"Well, Merry Christmas, Irving, Marshall, and Goldie," said Walter. "And a Merry Christmas to all the sleeping critters."

He headed down the hall to the cattery.

"Lotho blatho!" said Marshall.

Irving complained, "What is bugging you tonight, anyway?"

"Lotho blatho!"

"Say what you have to say *after* you've finished your dinner, please," said Irving.

Walter was in with the cats when the lights went up again and a voice said, "Honey? Walter? Where are you, darling?"

A Christmas miracle! Olivia Splinter had arrived.

She must have left the front door open, for there was an awful draft. Irving was concerned for Marshall, because snakes caught cold very easily.

There was no way, of course, to tell Walter's

mother that he was in the cat room.

Suddenly Goldie managed to nudge open the door of his cage, jump out, and race from the kennel.

"How did *you* get loose?" Olivia Splinter shouted after him. "Come back!"

"Lotho blatho!" Marshall tried again, and not until then did Irving realize the snake had somehow sensed that Walter had not fastened Goldie's cage. Marshall had been trying to warn them that Goldie could escape.

10

A Distasteful Secret

Jimmie so often worked on Christmas Day that she usually received her presents Christmas Eve.

"A diary!" said Jimmie. "I never had a diary!"

"Welcome to the Real World," said her father.

"I hope not," Jimmie replied. "I don't want to be a civilian."

"This diary goes from Christmas Day to Christmas Day, so you can begin writing in it tomorrow."

"What will I write about?"

"That's up to you. It's your personal diary with a little lock and key. Write about what little girls write about. Write about your life, your dreams, your worries . . . your boyfriends."

"Boyfriends?"

"Someday they'll be coming around."

"Ms. Fondaloot says I am not to worry, because she is paid to do the worrying and I am paid to do the work."

"That's just agent talk," said Mr. Twilight. "In the R.W. little girls don't have agents. *Most* little girls don't have agents."

"Ms. Fondaloot says I'm not like most little girls because I have talent."

"Yes, you do, but I want you to think seriously about another kind of life. Show biz will always be there, but these years when you're so young will go fast. Maybe you would be happier if you became more like other kids."

"I'm not unhappy the way you think I am," said Jimmie. "I don't want to be in the R.W. I miss Mom so bad I ache, but when I'm performing I feel close to her."

"I know, honey. But she'd want you to get a good education, meet kids your age, all the things she could never do when she was a child."

"Look how *she* turned out, though. I hope *I* become like Mom."

"I hope you do, too. . . . It's late. We'd better open the rest of our presents."

Outside, the snow was coming down hard.

"I hope we don't get snowed in, Dad. When there's a storm like this, Angel on High always takes a room in the city at the Y. What if StarStretch can't get here tomorrow?"

"Ms. Fondaloot will call if that seems likely."

Jimmie put the diary with her other gifts. Angel on High, who was in the Christmas show with Jimmie, had given her Roscoe the Robotic Frog from Manley Toy Quest. He came on a plastic lily pad, made a *ribbit!* noise, and threw out his red plastic tongue to catch the fly that came with him in the box.

While they opened their Christmas presents, Placido was batting a piece of tinsel on a lower branch of the tree Sam Twilight had lugged aboard the boat and trimmed a few hours ago.

Placido remembered the taste of tinsel from other Christmases before he had landed in Critters. Tinsel wasn't delicious, not like the mackerel he'd finally had to scarf down while Sam Twilight slept and waited for the girl to come aboard. But tinsel was fun to swallow. It was like rubber bands. It was like spaghetti strands.

Placido knew when he ate the tinsel, his secret could come out. Placido was a projectile vomiter. It was another reason that his adoptions did not work out. He might have used some restraint and left the tinsel on the tree, but he had an idea he would get seasick soon anyway. Why not enjoy himself while he could?

His second owner (Placido never discussed his first owner) used to hold her head whenever it happened and holler, "PLA-CI-DO! Oh, noooooooooo!" She was a high-strung opera singer who seemed to prefer Polly, her parrot. She was always asking Polly if she wanted a cracker in baby talk. She didn't talk that much to Placido because, she said, he did *all* the talking.

As a young and healthy Siamese, Placido *had* strolled about exercising his lungs, as Siamese like to do.

Polly would shout, "Shut the cat up! Shut the cat up!"

Sometimes when the diva went off to a performance, she would forget to lock Placido out of the kitchen.

Then Placido would jump up and cling to the cage and poke his head under the black silk cover.

"Madame de Flute!" the parrot would scream. "Madame de Flute!"

Placido would get the cage swinging fast. He

would leer at the parrot and hiss and yowl. The parrot would always faint, falling to a heap at the bottom of the cage.

When Madame de Flute got home, she would scold Placido and tell him she was going to give him away.

Placido never believed her until he found himself at Critters. The parrot had finally fought back. Polly had lost only a few garish green feathers. But Placido had lost his right blue eye and his home.

Placido didn't know how the girl would react to his secret. She was the one in charge of things—he could see that. Her Santa Claus father was a lonely man. All the while he was trimming their tree, he had sung Christmas carols in this melancholy tone that depressed even Placido, who rarely let things get him down. Twilight had even said "Oh Elaine, Elaine," in his sleep, still in his Santa Claus costume, during the long wait for Jimmie. Placido had sneaked in a brief catnap atop the pillows stuffed inside Twilight's pants.

Now Sam Twilight wore a handsome cashmere sweater the girl had just given him for Christmas.

"Let's get to bed," he told the girl. "You have four shows tomorrow . . . and don't you have another audition?"

"Not until after Christmas."

"How did it go with BrainPower?"

"I thought you'd never ask."

"If I ask, you always say Ms. Fondaloot does all your worrying. But I know better."

"I said 'consensus of opinion,' which is a major faux pas."

"I say it. Shouldn't I say it?"

"It's redundant."

"So just forget you said it. I remember that time your mother said 'irregardless' when we were at some townie's place for dinner. Someone told her that it wasn't even a word, and you would have thought she was caught with her hand in the till or caught naked or some other damn thing, the way she carried on. 'Oh, how could I have said that, Sam? Oh, Sam, how can you stand being with an ignoramus like me?' I said, 'Count your victories, Elaine. Don't sweat the small stuff.' And that's all it is, Jimmie. It's small stuff. It's not the only job in the world either."

"It's the best one I've ever been up for! Kids would be able to download me! I'd be a spokeskid!"

"Honey, a kid your age shouldn't have this stress. You should be laughing and playing."

"I play chess with Babe in the Manger."

"I'm talking about kids' games. Hide-and-seek. Pin

the tail on the donkey."

"I'm too old for those games, Daddy. I'm eleven!" said Jimmie. "I think it stresses *you* more than me."

"I know that's what you think, but you're wrong. I wouldn't care if you left show biz tomorrow."

"I may have to," Jimmie said, "if StarStretch can't get through the snow. Then I wouldn't have to work another Christmas Day. Angel on High is right! She says it's the pits to work on Christmas. It sucks! She says she'd like to tell them to go screw themselves!"

Her father heaved a sigh. "Don't *you* start sounding like Angel on High. Your mother winced at language like that. I thought of her all day while I was over at the Star-Tintrees'. She would have loved that house with the big tree, and the little girl, Sun Lily. She's about your age, I think. And listen to this: We've been invited to their New Year's Eve party."

"To perform, right?"

"Right. That's what we do. But they're a lovely family, and they've asked boys and girls from the Ross School. Wouldn't you like to have some nice, normal friends from the Real World?"

"Probably not," said Jimmie. "I wouldn't know what to say to them."

"That was your mother's problem too. She'd start

talking people's ears off about Jimmie Spheeris. Nobody'd ever heard of him *or* his music."

"Their loss," Jimmie said.

"I know that. But you don't want to grow up at a loss for words on social occasions."

"Daddy, look at the time! We need to get to bed right now!"

"At least we don't have to walk a cat," he said.

"Where is that cat?" she said.

Placido had fled to the master's cabin, a piece of tinsel hanging from his mouth. He had never trusted little girls. One he'd lived with for a few days had called him Pooty Wooty, forced him into doll clothes, and tried to wheel him around in a baby carriage. The scratch he gave her across her arm had him back inside the fake-leopard carrying case and on his way to Critters one more time.

So he *wasn't* perfect.

Placido favored the high shelf in the master's cabin, where he could oversee the aft deck from the porthole. He didn't have his sea legs yet, and he didn't like the way the boat rocked, because he had no claws to grip anything if a big wave rolled in.

There wouldn't be any waves for a while, not with the snow coming down and the bay water turning to ice.

From the shelf, in the daytime, he could see the gulls that perched on the railing, waiting for hand-outs. He liked to fall asleep in a sun spot while he daydreamed about snatching one of them.

His first night aboard, even though he could see only a few watery lights on the bay, he liked perching on the shelf, looking up at the stars, and the moon with its moody face, sometimes clouded, sometimes this huge circle of light so bright Placido watched it through his paws.

The girl and her father called out good night to each other, finally, and in the darkness there was no sound but the water gurgling under the boat and the wind blowing the snow.

Silent night, Placido thought as he curled up and closed his eyes. He dreamed of Roscoe the Robotic Frog sitting on his stupid plastic pad, saying *ribbit!* while his red plastic tongue darted out to catch the fly.

Placido slept with a tiny smile of anticipation tipping his furry mouth.

11

Wait for the Beep!

ow long was it before Placido was blasted out of his sleep by the sound of the telephone ringing?

Then the answering machine went on full pitch:

I'M THE SANTA CLAUS CLOWN—
I'M THE BEST CLOWN IN TOWN.
TO YOUR PARTY I'LL COME
FOR A REASONABLE SUM!

Placido had leaped down from the shelf, trembling from the shock of Sam Twilight's voice booming in the dark, quiet night.

LEAVE YOUR NUMBER AND NAME—
ENTERTAINING'S OUR GAME.
JIMMIE IS HERE TOO:
IF YOU WANT HER, SAY WHO.

Placido had heard that recording all day long.
Now they were both home, and there was no reason
for him to have to hear it yet again!

WAIT FOR THE BEEP
BEFORE YOU LET OUT A PEEP!

Placido covered his ears with his front paws.

Beeeeeeeeeeeeeeeeeeeep, the machine screamed, and
Placido rolled his eyes in agony.

"Hello? Hello? This is Mrs. Randall from Montauk.
We're so very sorry to call this late, but we can't find
the phone number you gave us for Critters. We're
desperate to find Rex! We want to leave a message in
case he's there. If we could have him for Christmas,
our little boy would be so happy! There's no listing in
the book for Critters. Thank heavens you gave us
your business card, Sam Twilight. Hello?"

Now Jimmie was awake and calling, "Daddy? Is
that Ms. Fondaloot? Am I supposed to go into New
York right now?"

"Hush, honey. It's not Ms. Fondaloot."

Mr. Twilight turned on a light, sat up in his bunk bed, and took the phone. "This is Sam Twilight. . . . It's all right. . . . Critters is listed as *Hamptons* Critters Shelter, but never mind. I'll give you the number again."

After he hung up, Sam Twilight began to tell Jimmie about the boy named Bob and the lost yellow Labrador retriever he'd heard of at the mall that day.

Goldie, Placido thought. Goldie!

Placido remembered when Goldie had first arrived at Critters on a cold afternoon, not too long ago. Placido had been taken out of the cat room to be groomed. He was in the Critters examination room, waiting for the girl with the brush and comb, when Goldie was brought in. Goldie needed a bath badly.

"My name is Placido. Welcome to Critters."

"I won't be here long," Goldie had said.

"Where have I heard that before?"

"I plan to escape," Goldie had said. "You'll see."

Placido had wished the dog luck and then purred hard, picturing a daring dog escape that would liven up the holidays.

Right before the groomer appeared, Goldie had told Placido, "My real name is Rex. Bob, my owner, named me. Do you know what Rex means?"

"King," Placido had answered. Placido was no dunce of a cat. He had lived with a diva, after all, and Madame Fleurette de Flute had sung many roles in many languages.

12
Heartbroken Family

hristmas Eve at the Uttergores'.

"How many lost-dog posters did you manage to get down?" Percival Uttergore asked his ailing sister when she came home crying from the cold.

"I found thirty," she said, "and I have twenty-nine in my car. I brought in this one for you to look at."

She put it on the table. The ink was running from the wet snow.

REWARD! LOST DOG!
Answers to Rex
Yellow Labrador retriever, 5 years old
Family heartbroken
Call 631.555.2868
REWARD! $$$$$$$$$$$

"Sometimes I wonder about people," said Percival Uttergore. "Imagine paying money to get a dog back!"

"Some people get great happiness from a pet," said Ursula.

"'Family heartbroken!'" Uttergore scoffed. Then, in an imitation of a distraught female, he whined, "Oh me oh my, me doggie is lost and me am heartbroken!"

Ursula wondered if she should proceed to the basement, where her brother had fixed a small room for her near the furnace. There were no dogs being held for rewards, only the clothesline with the leashes attached where they could walk when they were in residence.

Ursula knew her brother did not approve of Christmas celebrations, because they were just a waste of hard-earned money, but she held the hope that she might dry herself by the fire, this being a special night for some.

"The kind of people who get great happiness from a pet are the kind of people who have very little life," said Uttergore.

"Yes, Percival. I suppose you're right."

"Then why did you say some people get great happiness from a pet?"

"I'm too cold to think straight. I cannot feel my feet."

"They're there," he said. For a moment she had imagined he was consoling her, saying, "There, there," but she quickly realized he was talking about her feet being there.

"Tomorrow," said her brother, who had put his Barcalounger in the reclining position before the fire, "we'll drive around and see if we can find this Rex. Set your clock for seven A.M., Ursula, and this time I think I'll have my eggs over easy. Rye-bread toast. Bacon crisp. Coffee as usual. Good night."

"Good night."

"Be glad you don't live with someone who goes boo hoo hoo over an animal."

13

Racetrack Riffraff

Peke could not forget that on Christmas Eve he had been yelled at by Nell, all because of the greyhound.

His fitful slumber had been blessed with a dream that Percival Uttergore's red gloves had reached out for Catherine, and *pfffft*, she'd disappeared. Rich dog or poor dog, family dog or stray, you had at one time or another been told of the evil man who captured dogs. When a new dog was introduced to an only-dog household (even just as a visitor), what only dog did not dream of the dogcatcher coming to snatch the new arrival?

Now this lowlife had come in from a long morning walk with Ginny and Sun Lily, and she was tracking wet paw marks across the hall floor. On Christmas Day! Peke looked at her with utter disgust.

"Sorry," Catherine murmured to him.

"Save your apology," Peke told her. "It is too late! Because of you I was beaten on Christmas Eve."

"Nell didn't beat you. She barely raised her voice," Catherine said.

"No wonder they put you greyhounds to sleep after you can't race anymore," said Peke. "You're informers! *I* would never have told on *you*!"

"We're not informers," Catherine insisted. "They put us to sleep because they are cruel. They think just because we've never had any home life, we won't get along in people's homes."

"They're right about that," said Peke. "You don't know enough to keep your mouth shut!"

"I've kept my mouth shut, Peke. I know you have a secret place where you take ribbons and rubber dog bones and mittens. I've been watching you."

"You don't know where it is, though."

"I bet I can find it," said Catherine. "Let's bet the red rubber hot dogs that Sun Lily gave us for Christmas."

"It's a bet. And stay away from Sun Lily."

"Why should I stay away from her?"

"Because you're not family. You're the dregs."

"*She* doesn't act like I'm the dregs."

"Because she's polite. I don't happen to be. Sun Lily and I have a special bond, both of us having Chinese origins. You are from Critters, and before that you were from the racetracks. You have no breeding!"

In the kitchen Nell Star was talking on the telephone.

"We'll have to call the volunteers to start a search party," she was saying. "Goldie couldn't have gotten far. Oh, what a shame. Just when we may have located his owner, he bolted."

Catherine gnawed nervously on a chew stick.

Peke sighed. "Another lost dog! Ginny and Nell don't get any rest, not even on Christmas Day!"

"Don't you feel sorry for the lost dog too?" Catherine asked.

"You down-on-your-luck dogs bring trouble on everybody, including yourselves," Peke declared. "You *belong* at the dogcatcher's!" His small goldfish eyes had a very cross expression. The plume he had for a tail bristled. "You are the outcasts of society!" he continued. "I happen to be a direct descendent of Lootie, Queen Victoria's Pekingese!"

"Please get your face out of my face," said Catherine.

"Pekingese do not have faces!" Peke snarled. "We have masks. You would know that if you were not just racetrack riffraff!"

Catherine did not have an answer to that. Anyway, Catherine was worried now about what Nell had said on the telephone. Something about volunteers going out to look for Goldie.

How could Goldie have gotten loose?

As much as Catherine hated losing bets, she was glad she had lost her Christmas stocking to the Labrador retriever. Maybe he had eaten the doggie doughnuts in both stockings before taking off. Catherine didn't want to imagine Goldie running lost and hungry in the cold.

"Christmas with riffraff is no Christmas at all," Peke grumbled, waddling away from Catherine.

"You should be more sympathetic," Catherine called after him. "You're lucky to have such a nice home!"

"It won't be a nice home until you go back to Critters!" Peke barked over his shoulder.

14

Dear Diary

Christmas Day

Dear Diary,

Radio City Music Hall is a madhouse.

Outside, there are long lines waiting for the six-o'clock show.

Inside, all the talent is hanging out in various places—behind the 144-foot stage, upstairs in the rehearsal rooms, and down in the basement, where I am.

This year I appear at the very end of Act I, "Christmas in Central Park." I am onstage for four minutes, right before the thirty-six Rockettes storm out. Then I am onstage for two minutes with the dancing dwarfs in "Santa's Home," Act II.

Then again two minutes in the finale.

Now I am in one of the dressing rooms, soaking my feet. The actors from the Nativity Scene are hanging out here. The Three Kings of Orient are playing gin rummy on one side of me. Joseph and Mary are playing backgammon on the other side.

Next door the Rockettes get into their costumes for the March of the Wooden Soldiers.

I am supposed to be doing a homework assignment for online correspondence school. Write about something unique in a country was the lesson that came up on the computer last week.

I'm wearing the red kimono that belonged to Mom. In the pocket is the last photograph of her, holding Dancer. It was taken last summer just after we'd all closed in Nursery Rhymes. Mom was Mother Goose, her final role.

We were docked in Miami when I took that picture. Mom was sitting on the deck with Dancer in her arms. Dad had gone into town for supplies.

If she hadn't loved that dog so, she'd probably still be alive. When the hurricane roared into the harbor, we got off Summer Salt. But Mom called out, "I'm going back for Dancer!" The last time I saw them both, Mom was swimming toward Summer Salt. Dancer was huddled near a life preserver, shivering and yipping.

The Christmas card from Check and Shirley made me think of times in the rain we'd talk in the pie car. One time Check said what he liked was leaving to go someplace new. The train would move slowly at first, so you didn't feel it. Then you'd hear a click, feel a sway, and you were started, steel wheels over rails.

He said sometimes when you did something new in your life, there'd be a click, too, as you'd start to get it. Then you'd get it and pretty soon you'd be going fast. He said it was that way when he met Shirley, and I remember Shirley said, "Get out of here, we never went fast doing anything, including making our minds up to leave this freak show." She'd be smoking no hands, teasing him, saying it was a freak show, but we all knew she loved it.

The thing is I can't just go pffft from that world to the Real World.

Now I hear the lambs from the Nativity Scene baaing in their pen down the hall. There's an old donkey down there too, and other farm animals.

Dancer used to bark and bark at their smells and their sounds, but he was like Shirley. It was just noise he made. He loved it since he was a real back-lot dog, who knew just how close he could get to the big cats, the camels, the trucks, and the forklift.

But his barking would get the Sugar Plum Fairy mad. She would snarl, "Cork it!" Dewdrop, who led the Waltz of the Flowers, always said Sugar Plum was just jealous because Dancer got so much applause.

I made up my mind to forget all about flubbing the BrainPower audition. I am not going to blame myself anymore for saying "consensus of opinion."

"Five minutes!" a stagehand just shouted.

I've got to get into my white spangled tutu.

One of the Three Kings of Orient is fastening back his big ears with adhesive tape called Earies.

My heart pounds every time I listen to the sound of the Rockettes charging up the stairs.

No matter how many shows a day I do, I always get a charge when it's time to go on.

15

"Rex, This Is Rags, Can You Hear Me?"

Some cats think and dream in poetry.

People believe cats lie around all day and do nothing important, but some cats are very busy composing verse.

Such a cat was Rags Randall, a coon cat from Montauk.

He had several poems that were his favorites, and as he sat in the window looking outdoors, he recited one or two.

His very favorite was called "Gifts."

> I like to crush the mouses' bones.
> I like to eat their hearts.
> I like upon the doormat
> To leave their other parts.

I wait for mouses in the fields,
I catch them by the toes.
A mouse's tail is always peeled.
Put mustard on the nose.

Of course there were others about birds and moles, chipmunks and rabbits, the frustrations of winter and the joys of warm weather. There was even one about the big fat Persian cat next door who had gross mats in her hair because her owner did not know enough to comb her every day.

But Rags had never written a poem about Rex until that Christmas Day.

Cats rarely write about dogs, no matter how desperate they might be for material. Why remind themselves of what life is like with a dog around?

Even when a dog tries to be pleasant, as Rex always did, what is more deplorable than the sound of a dog barking just as you have slipped into the sort of deep sleep that finds you flopped on your back with your paws up, your whiskers drooping, your tongue hanging out?

Then . . . *Woof! Woof! Woof!*

Nothing more than a car going down the street, and for that you are jolted out of your sweet slumber!

Five other obnoxious things dogs do:

1. Come in from the rain shaking themselves near your cat bed!

2. Return from a walk stinking of manure (and once it was skunk)!

3. Gallop through the fields looking for you just as you are sneaking up on a vole!

4. Hog the rug in front of the fireplace on cold nights!

5. Try to knock your food bowl off the table and gobble it down!

Rags could go on and on. There wasn't a cat alive who did not compare himself to dogs again and again. There wasn't a cat alive who did not marvel at the difference, raise his eyes to the heavens, and utter, *"Dogs!"* with the same tone reserved for ticks, fleas, and baths.

But on this Christmas Day Rags would not care what disagreeable thing Rex did, if only he could be there to do it.

Rags was heartsick, sleepless, and unable to finish his Fancy Feast, even when it was beef and giblets, the flavor he loved best.

He sat by the window looking out forlornly. He was face-to-face with a grackle, and his teeth were not even chattering.

His creative juices were soured with grief.

Rex, this is Rags, can you hear me?
I miss not having you near me.
Run fast, Rex, run hard,
Till you come to our yard!
Rex, this is Rags, can you hear me?

16
Tinsel Turds

By the day after Christmas, Placido had his sea legs. He padded through the boat with a sure step on a regular route that led to the master's cabin. There he devoured Roscoe the Robotic Frog's red plastic tongue. He chewed up his voice box, too, so he could not cry *ribbit!* It took Placido a long time to accomplish all this.

From the porthole Placido could see that one saucy seagull who often perched on the aft deck, waiting for handouts.

Placido had named him Snack, for that was what he would be one of these days when Placido could figure out a way to reach him.

* * *

In the main cabin the girl was sitting at the computer. Her father was getting into his overcoat. They were still discussing the composition she was to write about something unique in a country.

"Why can't you write about Miami?" her father asked. "You really know Miami!"

"But the United States isn't known for something in Miami!"

"Remember the summer your mom, me, and you played San Antonio? There's a fascinating city for you: San Antonio, Texas!"

"That's not what they mean, Daddy! That's like naming *me* for a famous person, instead of someone who's a big star."

"You're a big star! You just played Radio City Music Hall, for pete's sake. And don't sell San Antonio short! Remember the Alamo! That was San Antonio!"

"They want a country, something unique. They want Italy, or France, or England! Someplace exotic! And I am *not* a star, Daddy! I didn't even get a callback from BrainPower!"

"Well, you're not in a good mood this morning, are you, Jimmie? I have to go buy lumber to repair the aft deck. It's rotting. . . . Try to cheer up. New Year's is coming, and we have the Star-Tintree date."

After he left, the girl went back to the master's cabin and began talking to Placido.

"If I was going to get another chance to try out for Jane Brain, I'd have heard by now."

She was sitting in the captain's chair while Placido jumped away from the porthole, down to the bed.

"I wouldn't have been a good Jane Brain anyway. I said 'consensus of opinion,' Placido!"

Placido suddenly found himself purring contentedly, for he had never had an owner who confided in him.

Madame de Flute had sung opera to him sometimes, but more often she made threats like: "Stay away from Polly's cage, Placido, or you're toast!"

And of course there were all the owners after Madame de Flute (Placido never discussed his first owner), the two-month owners, the two-week owners, the two-day owners, and the two-hour owners. Placido could hear them yelling at him.

"Get down, Placido!"

"If you don't eat what's there, then you'll starve!"

"Get that dead mouse out of here!"

"Don't paw your litter so hard—it's all over the floors!"

"Placido, do you hear me calling you?"

"Placido! You puked on my new cashmere sweater!"

"I'd rather be Twinkle Toes than Jane Brain, anyway," the girl continued. "But let's face it, without Dancer I'm not special anymore."

She was beginning to cry. Even better than a stick of butter, Placido enjoyed licking salty tears. He jumped from the bed and sat beside her on the desk. She made no attempt to pick him up, so forget salty tears. Maybe she was repulsed by the eyehole minus the eye. Maybe she was just like everyone else: not taken with him for whatever reason. Just when he was beginning to think of her as Jimmie, too, even though this time he had promised himself to keep his distance from whoever adopted him. Placido was not spoiling for another rejection.

Behind her there were framed photographs lined up: a woman, a woman and the girl, a woman and the man, and one of that stupid little Boston terrier with his eyes popping out of his head and his stubby tail.

"I wish we were in Miami, where it's warm." The girl sniffled. "If you go back to Miami with us, you'll be able to sit out on the deck and sunbathe, Placido."

If. Right? *If.* There was always an if in life, wasn't there?

If you have his claws removed, he won't ruin the furniture.

Remember that if?

Major surgery was performed on him, just to save the arms on some ratty old sofa.

And what had this famous decorator done when Placido showed her his forgiveness by presenting her with a bloody crow kicking and biting as he pounced on it and then wrestled it through the pet door with his teeth? She had called him a killer. Never mind her flyswatter, her mousetraps, her Roach Motels—*Placido* was the killer! Another trip back to Critters!

The girl was sounding sadder and sadder, and she got on a talking jag next—about guess who? Dancer!

Dogs, Placido mused, will do anything—even humiliate themselves—to please people.

You would never catch a cat waltzing around on his hind legs!

Neither would you catch one jumping up and down, making a racket that would raise the dead, barking until his throat hurt, just because some people were visiting Critters.

"Oh, take me home! Oh, adopt me!" they'd cry out shamelessly.

They had no pride, dogs didn't!

Both Placido and the girl jumped at the sound of knocking on the door.

"It's too late for the mailman," said the girl. "Maybe it's FedEx. Maybe the BrainPower people wrote instead of calling."

She was on her feet.

The knocking became louder.

A dog, of course, would have gone ballistic, barking and tearing toward the door to see who it was. But that was not the way of a cat.

Placido glared up at Dancer's photograph on the shelf by her desk.

He heard the door open, and he heard the girl say, "Oh. It's you."

Then she said, "You can come in and see for yourself. So far he's knocked over our tree and made tinsel turds."

"You don't sound like you're mad for him anymore. You sound like you're mad *at* him."

"I just don't know if he likes it here or not."

Neither does *he*, Placido thought. How was he supposed to like being second fiddle to a dead Boston terrier? Placido brushed his paw against the framed photograph of Dancer.

"I took the bus all the way out to see him," said

the boy. Placido knew that voice. Placido liked that voice. That was Mrs. Splinter's grandson, Walter the Worry Wart.

"Did you have a nice Christmas, Jimmie?"

"I worked. Working on Christmas sucks."

"My mother came for an hour Christmas Eve. She couldn't stay longer because of the storm. She didn't want to get stuck."

"Where is your father?" Jimmie asked.

The world-famous globe-trotter, Placido called him. Guy Splinter broadcasting from anywhere but where his family was. Sometimes when Mrs. Splinter came to Critters early in the morning, the dogs would hear him talking on the *Today* show. Word would spread that Guy Splinter was here, there, everywhere but his home.

Walter told the girl his father had been in Israel. "But he's on his way back. He's getting an apartment in New York City! Just when I'm in so much trouble!" he said. "It was my fault a dog got loose. I didn't fasten his cage. I'm so worried that Mr. Uttergore will find him!"

Placido gave the picture of Dancer a little push.

"Placido! You have a visitor!"

Then another little push.

"So long, Popeyes," Placido whispered. "Roscoe

the Robotic Frog is waiting for you."

The dancing dog disappeared down the crack between the desk and the wall just as Jimmie and Walter reached the master's cabin.

"You have company, Placido."

"He's purring," Walter said. "He seems pretty pleased with life."

17

Days of Rugs and Couches

Two days after Christmas Marshall was swinging from the plastic tree branch inside his cage. All the other cages in the row were empty. Goldie was still missing. Catherine was still at the Star-Tintrees'. And Dewey, the red Irish setter, had been adopted the day after Christmas.

To make matters more grim, there was a new critter, who looked like a cross between a pig and a pit bull. She was hairless, save for a fuzzy little Mohawk between her ears. Even Marshall, who had a fondness for big words, could not pronounce her breed. Xoloitzcuintle, which was pronounced *SHO-lo-EETS-queen-tlee*. Mrs. Splinter had already invited a professional dog breeder to see this four-legged freak, now named Posh, because the breeder said she could cost a thousand dollars and up and she was fast becoming the new fashionable dog. Already her kind was appearing in the pages of *Elle* and *Vogue* magazines.

Her cage was put near Marshall's because she, too, was susceptible to colds and needed the extra heat from the radiator.

Posh had been brought to Critters because her owner had been arrested for grand theft while trying to remove some mink coats from the checkroom of the Women's Exchange. Of course Posh was humiliated and embarrassed, and therefore barked twenty minutes out of sixty every hour except at darkest night. She also cried. Marshall was astonished to see dripping tears roll down her leathery cheeks. When Marshall made an attempt to introduce himself, she turned away, her nose wiggling with mortification.

Days of Our Lives was playing on the television in the office, but Mrs. Splinter was not there to watch her favorite soap opera. It was Irving's favorite, too. He often watched it through the mirror, just as he watched adoption interviews. But Irving was out with Mrs. Silverman, the volunteer who always walked him in the afternoon.

Marshall could see Mrs. Splinter coming out of

the supply room with Mrs. Tintree, whom everyone called Flo. Mrs. Splinter was giving Catherine's ragged brown sweater to her.

"Poor Catherine is *never* warm enough," said Flo. "Ginny and Nell want to keep Catherine for good, if Peke will accept her. Everyone is trying so hard to find Goldie, we'll definitely keep Catherine until after New Year's. That way you'll have one less critter to care for."

Marshall's forked tongue quivered as the pair came closer. He had always hidden when Flo was in Critters. He had the idea she would go ape if she came upon a snake, so many visitors did, particularly the senior citizens.

He decided he was not going to move. Let her get a big scare! Good for the circulation to have fresh adrenaline zap the system. He waited to hear the usual "Eeeeeeeeeek! A snake!" How many times had he heard that?

But Flo Tintree surprised him, calling out in a melodious voice, "My my my my my! What have we here?"

"A lovely king snake," said Mrs. Splinter.

"Oh, he *is* a lovely snake," said Flo Tintree. "I never knew you had a snake back here."

"I have to keep him near the radiators," said

Mrs. Splinter. "He has to be warm at all times. Snakes catch cold very easily."

"Oh, my! *Do* keep him warm. What does he eat?"

"Frozen mice, mostly, though he prefers live rats my grandson sometimes brings him from Animal House. He would eat another snake as well."

"So you are a cannibal," Flo Tintree said to Marshall. "Oh, my my my!"

But she did not seem to be saying it with distaste; it sounded more like amusement. Marshall liked that, because he also found amusement in cannibalism. Eating his own kind wasn't always a meal of survival. Sometimes it simply hit the spot.

Now, very, very, very few visitors to Critters ever spoke to Marshall unless they were children. Adults spoke about him ("Eeeeeeeeeek! A snake!"), but they never looked him in the eye and spoke directly to him.

Marshall felt a tiny thrill of pleasure run the course of his twisted body. He could not wait for Irving to return from his walk so he could tell him.

Then Mrs. Splinter said, "Now for the pièce de résistance! Here is our newest acquisition, a rare breed. Xoloitzcuintle. Xolo for short. But have you ever seen anything like her?"

"Never!" Mrs. Tintree sucked in her breath, let it out. "Never!"

"We call her Posh."

"Oh, and she is indeed posh."

"The famous artists Frida Kahlo and Diego Rivera owned xolos."

"Fascinating. *Fascinating*," said Mrs. Tintree. "Oh, thank you for pointing her out to me."

When Irving returned, he came back early, grumbling and lumbering about in his cage.

"What's wrong?" Marshall asked the pointer.

"My arthritis is kicking in. This cold cement floor isn't good for an old fellow."

"Something exquisitely exciting just happened to me!" Marshall boasted, but Irving was too grumpy to hear about anything exquisitely exciting.

Irving said, "Dewey is older than I am, in case anyone should ride up on a bicycle and ask you. How did *he* get adopted? And how does that pig bull rate a warm spot?"

"Something exquisitely exciting—"

But Irving cut him off again. "Mrs. Silverman said, 'We should not let our fears hold us back from pursuing our hopes.' She said that was from a speech by the thirty-fifth president of the United States: John F. Kennedy."

"And look what happened to *him*!" said Marshall,

peeved because he could not seem to share his news with the pointer. "So much for fearless living."

Irving flopped down on the floor of his cage and let out a long, sad sigh. "People have their troubles too—you are right, Marshall. If they're not getting shot down, they get frozen shoulder, which Mrs. Silverman has, and she is also feeling knee pain. She says the knees are the first thing to go."

"Irving, I am trying to tell you something, but you are interested in everyone but me, it seems. I am trying to tell you that not five minutes ago Flo Tintree spoke to me for a most enjoyable interlude."

"Exquisitely exciting," Irving murmured sarcastically.

"Yes, it was! Don't you realize how seldom anyone speaks to me? The trouble with being a snake is that people aren't inclined to talk with you."

"Walter always talks to you," said Irving.

"Walter is a small boy, and sometimes small boys *do* stop to chat. But I can't hang here waiting for Walter to pop by anymore. His grandmother has told him to stay away from the kennel from now on."

"He won't, though," said Irving. "You know Walter. He'll sneak in to check on things."

"You should have listened to my warning," said Marshall. "Goldie would be here now."

"'Lotho blatho' is not a warning. It is gibberish," Irving snapped. "You should have spat out that mouse's corpse and made your warning clear! Then I could have barked and gotten Walter's attention."

"When a snake swallows something, it doesn't come back up. I am not Placido! I am not a one-eyed Siamese. I am a king!"

Marshall unwound himself from the tree branch and dropped down into his wood chips.

He said, "Where is the boy who yearns to have a snake of his own? Without Walter around, I have no one who will tell me his secrets."

Irving said, "I think Walter misses his mother."

"My mother left me when I was just an egg," said Marshall. "She never visited me on weekends or came around at Christmas. She was gone for good!"

"I'm sorry to hear that, Marshall."

"I never gave it a thought," said Marshall. "I was off catching grasshopper larvae when I was one week old. We snakes don't miss our mothers."

"What I miss are the comforts of home," said Irving. "My poor old bones hurt on this hard cement floor!"

Marshall said, "Your days of rugs and couches are over, Irving. Neither one of us is ever going to get adopted. The old and the twisted aren't appealing to people, you know."

Irving's nose pressed against the bars of his cage. He said, "Will Posh ever shut up? Her barking is getting louder and louder!"

"Because someone's coming," said Marshall with his tongue throbbing.

Then Mrs. Splinter's voice called out from the office. "Come in! The door is open! May I help you?"

"I'm Bob Randall from Montauk. We talked on the phone Christmas Day about the yellow Labrador retriever I lost."

"Goldie!" Mrs. Splinter exclaimed.

"Rex is his real name," said the boy. "My mother's outside in the car with my little sister. We came to see if there's any word about Rex."

"Not yet, Bob. I'm sorry."

"Oh, this is sad," said Irving: "This is right out of *Days of Our Lives*."

18
Life Aboard *Summer Salt II*

There was no sign of Snack the seagull.

The man was out there on the aft deck pounding nails, his breath puffing out little clouds in the cold afternoon air.

Placido and the girl were inside, where there was a visitor: Ms. Fiona Fondaloot.

Ms. Fondaloot paraded about in her black Prada pants and her black suede three-inch-heel boots, smoking long thin brown cigarettes. The smoke was permeating every crevice inside *Summer Salt II*, and Placido was blinking his eyes against this invasive fog.

He was perched on the table watching while Ms. Fondaloot unscrewed her Mont Blanc pen.

"If you can't be Jane Brain, because you spoke out of turn," she said in her rich Russian-accented baritone, "perhaps you'll be right for the Ballbat cookie commercial. Slip into this, Jimmie."

"It looks like a sleeping bag, Fiona."

"It's good velvet. Don't rip it. It was lent to me as a favor, so you can get used to it before the audition. I do a lot of extra things for you, you know, because your mother crossed over."

"I wish you'd just say 'died.' She *died*."

"I never say 'died,'" said Ms. Fondaloot. She began writing on the long yellow pad with the blue lines across it. "I'll write down the address of Dolla, Dolla, and Dolla so you can give it to the limo driver tomorrow. The Ballbat client will be there at eleven. You be on time."

The girl got into the dark-brown costume and pulled up the zipper.

"I can't move!" she complained. "Does the client know how well I sing and dance?"

"You're a cookie crumb, darling. You don't dance. You curl up in that with your head covered."

As soon as the fresh ink was applied to the yellow paper with its blue lines, Placido marched across and sat down on it.

"That's going to cost that cat his butt!" Ms.

Fondaloot hollered, trying to swat Placido as he jumped back.

"YYYYYEEEEEEEEOW!" Placido exaggerated.

"What are you doing to him?" the girl cried out.

"He's smeared the address!"

"Don't hurt him!"

Don't hurt him? Placido nearly swooned at the sound of fear in the girl's voice. She did care about him after all! Jimmie liked Placido!

"I won't hurt him," said Ms. Fondaloot. "I'll kill him if I ever get my hands on him! He did that deliberately!"

"He was playing, Fiona."

"Not *that* cat. He has no game in him. They don't when they come from nothing," she said. "What is your father *doing*, Jimmie?"

"The aft deck is rotting," said the girl. "Daddy's fixing it."

"Jimmie, you've got to get your head inside the costume too. . . . Get that ugly cat out of here!"

Ugly, was he? Placido stomped back to the master's cabin. As much as he hated the sound of the hammering coming from that direction, he tolerated it. One had to have priorities, and right at the moment Placido's was to nap atop Ms. Fondaloot's black cashmere coat there on the bunk.

Have a hairy New Year, Ms. Fondaloot!

Placido would probably dream of Snack, as usual, but he would not mind at all if he dreamed, instead, of Jimmie.

19
Coming?

"What a beautiful Lab you are!" said the lady. "Come here, boy, don't be afraid. . . . Someone must have abandoned you. Did someone leave you in the woods?"

She was crouching near him, one glove off, beckoning to him.

Goldie was sitting there trembling from the cold and hunger. He had been followed for a while by a brown Bronco with P U on the license plate. When a large, shaggy-haired man finally parked and got out, Goldie saw the red gloves. Every dog at Critters had warned against those gloves. Goldie had headed into the woods, even though he had to high-step his way between the trees. His Critters tags caught on a tree branch and came off his neck. Now he was just this shivering anonymity.

"I had a dog like you once," said the lady. She was bundled up in a down coat with a plaid scarf. "His name was Elio. Come to me, boy."

Goldie wagged his tail.

"That's right. I won't hurt you. You know I won't hurt you."

Goldie watched her as she came toward him very slowly.

"You have no collar. Poor boy. Someone deserted you. How could someone do that?" She reached out and petted his head. "Come along with me, boy."

Exhausted, almost ready to give up hope of ever seeing Bob again, Goldie went with her.

20

The Girl with Four Mothers

When the swanky white stretch limo stopped in front of the house, Mrs. Tintree said, "Who could that be?"

"I'll go," said Sun Lily, rousing the dogs, who were intent on going too.

"Put a coat on."

"I'm not cold."

Catherine was. Catherine always was. She shivered behind Sun Lily as they went toward the car. Of course Peke was right behind Catherine. These days, if you wanted to know where Peke was, he was following the greyhound, the way a policeman shadowed the steps of a suspect. Peke was on territorial alert. If he did not protect his turf, who would?

The chauffeur ran around and opened the door for a girl just about Sun Lily's size. They were different in other ways. The stranger's hair was long and blond. Sun Lily's was dark and ear length. The stranger had a Walkman over her head and jeans on with Adidases. Sun Lily wore the new red Runway pants and jacket she'd gotten for Christmas.

The chauffeur was supposed to ring the bell and tell whoever answered the door that he was delivering the Magic House for the New Year's Eve performance. He was not happy about it; he was grumbling that the stop was not written on his ticket.

"Hello?" the stranger called out. "We have the Magic House."

"I'm Sun Lily Star-Tintree. What does this magic house do?"

"You'll see at the party. I'm Jimmie Twilight. We're just dropping it off."

"Are you famous?" Sun Lily asked.

Jimmie slipped the Walkman from her head to her shoulders and said, "Where did you get that idea?"

"From your father. He said you were a star."

"That's why I'm on my way to New York to try out as a cookie crumb." She laughed, and so did Sun Lily. Catherine's tail pounded the ground, but Peke scolded her for listening to the girls' conversation. Peke declared it was about New Year's Eve, a family celebration, not for Catherine's ears.

Sun Lily told Jimmie, "I'm not famous either, but I've been to China. Were you ever there?"

"The farthest away I've ever been is to Canada."

"I saw the Great Wall of China. It took ten years to build, and a million people were forced to work on it day and night. . . . What are you listening to on your radio?"

"I'm listening to a CD. I'm listening to a song called 'Snakeman.'"

Sun Lily clapped her hands. "Hey, one of my mothers was born in the year of the snake! Do you know the animal sign for your birth year?"

"No. I hope it's not a snake. I don't like them. My astrological sign is Gemini."

"I'm Virgo. If you come inside and meet three of my mothers, then I can find out your animal."

"There isn't time," said Jimmie. "How many mothers did you say you have?"

"I have four. I have Ginny Tintree, my real mother; I have Nell Star, my godmother; I have Grandma Flo, my grandmother; and in China somewhere is my birth mother."

"My mother died. But you met my father."

"He said he liked being Santa Claus, and he was once a professional clown."

"We both were. And my mother's family was with the circus for generations. This CD I've been listening to? It's Jimmie Spheeris. He was a circus kid too. He wrote songs like 'Lost in the Midway' and 'The Dragon Is Dancing' . . . and that's where 'Snakeman' came from too."

"'The Dragon Is Dancing'? Like Chinese New Year?"

Jimmie shrugged. "It could be." She took the Walkman off and handed it to Sun Lily. "You can hear his songs, and I'll get them back New Year's Eve."

"Oh, thank you! You're very kind, Jimmie."

"Not really."

"You aren't kind?"

Jimmie blushed. "I don't know *what* I am sometimes."

"I don't always know either," said Sun Lily. "Sometimes I think I might want to be a doctor."

The chauffeur was pushing the Magic House inside the front door.

They stood there watching him a moment.

Peke was in a big snit, not only about Catherine listening to personal conversations, but now about this chauffeur who had just marched up the sidewalk as though he were part of the family too. How dare he go in the front entrance!

Peke began to scold him with sharp, snarling barks.

"Peke! Peke!" Sun Lily called out. "Hush!"

Now the chauffeur was heading back from the house.

"I'm going to have to go, Sun Lily," Jimmie said.

Peke would show the chauffeur what he thought of him. He lifted his leg against the limo's front tire.

"Get outa there!" the driver yelled, running toward him. He gave Peke a kick that sent him a few feet into the air.

"Help! Help!" Peke yelped.

Sun Lily cried out, "No! No!"

Next thing, Catherine bounded forward with her yellow teeth flashing, just managing to catch the sleeve of the driver's uniform before he got inside the limo. There was the sound of cloth ripping and a furious chauffeur cursing.

Sun Lily clapped her hands. "Good for you, Catherine!"

"Is your little dog hurt?" Jimmie asked.

"He'll be all right, thanks to Catherine."

Sun Lily walked over to the limousine and asked

the chauffeur if he was hurt.

"That dog could have taken my arm off!" said the chauffeur.

"But she didn't. She didn't even bite you," Sun Lily said. "Don't you know you shouldn't ever kick an animal?"

"You tell Ms. Twilight I'll go without her if she doesn't get back in right now!"

"He's not going to hold the door open for me," Jimmie told Sun Lily. "He's terrified of Catherine."

"I love her so. I wish we could keep her, but Peke doesn't want her around," Sun Lily said.

"I had a dog named Dancer," said Jimmie. "He wouldn't let any other dog near me."

The chauffeur honked the horn, a long, loud blast.

Jimmie Twilight said, "I've got to split, babes."

"Good-bye," Sun Lily said. "Thanks for the music! I'll see you New Year's Eve! Good luck being a crumb!"

21

"Where Did the Little Crumb Come From?"

"Hi! Are you trying out for one of the dancing base-balls?"

"I'm trying out for the cookie crumb," Jimmie told him.

"I'm Cole Cane."

"I'm Jimmie Twilight."

"I was a germ in a toilet once."

"You're just saying that," Jimmie said.

"No, I was. I had to sing 'Whitewater stops the stink in your toilet and in your sink.'"

"You were in a little boat, with a paddle. I remember that ad!"

"'Paddle past the awful smell, paddle past the scum as well.'" He laughed. "I'm on my second call

113

for Ballbat," he said. "Are you with Boss Models?"

Jimmie said, "My agent sent me here. I'm not a real model yet."

"I was with Boss for a year, but I switched to Ford. I've done over a hundred jobs in sixteen months."

"What kind of jobs?"

"I was the Rope Slacks sailor and the Turton Tuna."

"'Be certain it's Turton.'"

"Right!" said Cole Cane. "I did print ads for Kmart, Gottex, DKNY, and the Gap."

"Wow!"

"Yeah. Fierce! And I'm up for a Calvin Klein jeans campaign to be shot by Steven Meisel!"

Jimmie said, "I was up for Jane Brain of BrainPower Limited."

"I was up for the part of Art Smart, but that creep Quick said I looked too loopy to have a thought in my head."

"He didn't like me because I said 'consensus of opinion,'" Jimmie said.

"What's wrong with saying that?"

"It's redundant," Jimmie said.

"Hey, Jimmie, I remember you now. I saw you last year. You danced with this great dog."

"Dancer."

"At Radio City! He was something!"

"Wasn't he?"

"I sing and dance myself, but in commercials. I decided to model rather than act right now, because the money is in modeling. If I save enough money, I'll go to Yale. I'll go to the drama school they have there."

"I think I'm too short to model," said Jimmie.

"Chase Cutler is short."

"Who's she?" Jimmie said.

"She's with Ford. She has freckles the size of lima beans down her back to her butt, but she covers them with makeup. She does a lot of work. She's about your age, thirteen, fourteen."

"I'm eleven. How old are you?"

"Guess."

"Sixteen? Seventeen?"

"I'm fourteen."

"You don't look it."

"Thanks."

Ms. Fondaloot arrived and put a protective arm around Jimmie's shoulders. "Don't let Cole Cane make you nervous," she whispered to Jimmie.

"He doesn't."

"I knew him when his mother was taking him around to cattle calls for background crowds. Now he's hot, but he's not that hot!"

"I like him."

"He and the chorus have all the lines, but never mind, cupcake. Work is work."

"I don't say *anything*?"

"I warned you! This is what happens when you speak out of turn! You're the crumb, cupcake. You just stay put, and remember to keep your head inside until the chorus sings. Then you poke your head out whenever you hear the words 'like some.' You look ashamed. You duck your head back inside. Got it?"

"Why can't *I* say 'like some'?"

"Because it's not in the script!"

"No lines at all?"

"What do you want, cupcake? You might have had a job with Mr. Quick. But you had to go and say 'consensus of opinion'!"

Jimmie was zipped up into her costume while Cole got into a baseball suit and cap. Three girls dressed as dancing baseballs were standing by an oversized cookie package.

Cole Cane picked up a ball bat.

After Jimmie got her head all the way under the brown velvet, someone shouted "Action!"

The dancing baseballs began to sing.

"Where did the little crumb come from?
Not from a Ballbat cookie!
It was not from a Ballbat peanut butter big fat
    raisin cookie . . ."

Then Cole Cane sang out in a deep voice (for someone fourteen!):

"Because Ballbat peanut butter big fat
Raisin cookie eaters don't
Ever leave a crumb!"

Then the chorus:

"Like some!"

Jimmie's head popped up.

"Like some!"

Jimmie's head disappeared.

As the chorus began all over again, a voice called, "Cut!"

Then another voice came through the bullhorn. "The cookie crumb's eyes are too wide and too big!"

"Squint, cupcake!" Ms. Fondaloot shouted.

"There's no time for that. Next!"

The wardrobe woman was hustling Jimmie out of her costume.

"This has animal hair on it!" the woman complained.

"How could it have animal hair on it?" Ms. Fondaloot said. "I have no animals!"

"Fiona, it's the last time you take something home from wardrobe!"

"Next!" came the shout again.

A redheaded girl was waiting for the brown velvet costume.

On her way back to East Hampton in the StarStretch limo, Jimmie wrote:

Dear Diary,

Dad is right about one thing, I guess. I don't have such a normal life when it comes to meeting boyfriends. I will probably never see Cole Cane again. Not that it matters all that much. In the R.W. so far I've only met one boy, and he's way into animals. I mean, way, way in. I'd have to crawl around on four legs to get his attention, if I wanted it. . . . Shall I tell you that I didn't make it even as a cookie crumb?

22

Secret Powers Cats Have

"Here, Rags, kitty kitty kitty!" Mrs. Randall called.

Rags was up in a tree in the blue of late afternoon, looking down at her.

"Where are you, Rags?"

He closed his eyes, and his tail swished.

He concentrated on Rex.

He used all the secret powers cats have to try and send his message to the dog.

Rex, this is Rags, I'm a mess!
I'm desperate and under great stress!

Mrs. Randall called louder, "KITTYKITTY-KITTYKITTY! RAGS!"

Avoid all gloves red—
You don't want to be dead!
Rex, you come home now, Rags said!

23

"Your Nose Is a Peanut."

oldie, who was once Rex, was now Elio.

But Goldie, who was once Rex and was now Elio, did not know what the lady wanted when she sat down at the piano and played "Chocolate."

"'*Bate, bate, chocolate, tu nariz de cacahuate.*' Sing along, Elio! Come on! '*Uno, dos, tres, Cho! Uno, dos, tres, Co! Uno, dos, tres, La! Uno, dos, tres, Te!*' Elio, come on! Sing along!"

Goldie kept wagging his tail and looking up at her expectantly. What did she want?

"You don't know Spanish, is that it? Okay. 'Stir, stir, chocolate, your nose is a peanut. One, two, three—' Can't you sing with me?"

Earlier that day when a visitor had rung the bell,

Goldie had raced around looking for something to retrieve. For that was his way when he lived with Bob. He would find something to carry to the door whenever a caller came. A bone, his leash, a glove, a ball.

He had found a pillow and carried it proudly to greet the lady's visitor.

"What are you doing, Elio?" she cried out. "Put that down! That's my good pillow! You are a bad boy!"

Goldie did not understand why she had not smiled at him or said to the visitor, "He's greeting you."

Now she brought her hands down hard on the piano keys and sighed. "You just don't sing, do you?"

Sing? A dog sing?

She was trying so hard to be a good owner, making a bed for him near her own, brushing him, hugging him.

"My Elio could sing!" Her voice broke. She was near tears.

Goldie sat there looking at her. He had never known a singing dog, nor a Spanish-speaking one. Elio must have been a very smart dog!

A small Christmas tree with blinking lights stood on a nearby table.

She shook her head sadly. "Oh, my poor, poor baby. My Elio."

Goldie knew what she was going through, for he longed for Bob. He wouldn't even have minded if Bob's baby sister had toddled up to him and pulled his ears. He just wished he were home.

Then the lady looked down at Goldie and said, "Do you want to go for a walk?"

He jumped up and shook his head.

She had put a collar with tags on him, and the tags jingled.

She got out a leash, and they set off from the trailer.

They went down a long path and came to water.

It was not an ocean. It was quiet water.

Goldie could remember the sound of the ocean, the waves slapping the beach. The Randalls loved Long Island, and before they'd moved here, they'd visited every summer. Bob would let him run free along the sand. Goldie would take off! But he would always look over his shoulder to be sure Bob was coming.

"Not so fast, Elio!" said the lady.

He felt the jerk to his collar that told him he was doing something he shouldn't, so he slowed up.

He heard her sigh again.

He knew that sigh well from hearing it in Critters. It was the sigh of longing for someone who was gone forever. Dewey, the Irish setter, had sighed that way again and again, and Marshall had told Goldie that Irving used to sigh that way.

Goldie kept his face down against the cold afternoon wind, and they plodded along.

Goldie remembered how Rags sometimes went out and climbed the tree in the front yard.

Bob's mother would call Rags and call him, and all the time the cat would be sitting up on a high branch looking down at her.

Then Goldie would be let out to look for her.

He would sit under the tree, barking.

"So that's where you are, Rags!" Bob would say.

And later, when Rags finally came down and they all went inside, Rags would say— But then the strangest thing happened in the middle of this memory of Rags.

Goldie could hear Rags saying something. It was not Rags' usual crabby tone scolding Goldie for some offense. It was Rags telling him to avoid all gloves red.

Goldie gave a bark of alarm.

The lady said, "Do you hear something, Elio?"

Goldie barked again.

"What do you want?" She sounded irritated.

She jerked his collar again.

The vision of Rags up in the tree disappeared,

and so did the sound of his mewing advice.

Goldie heeled obediently as they walked along by the bay. He could not see the brown Bronco chugging very slowly along the parallel road.

24

A Future with Lot Lice?

Placido looked as though he were drooling over Snack, which he did most mornings, but there was something more important on his mind than the taste of seagull. In fact, he did not even know what seagull tasted like, whether it would be more like chipmunk or closer to bluejay. But Placido knew very well what it was like to be returned to Critters, and that was where his thoughts were, suddenly, as the New Year approached. His one eye was on Snack, but his attention was on the conversation behind him, between Jimmie and her father.

"With BrainPower out of the picture, there's nothing holding us here, Jimmie. So after New Year's, why don't we sail down to Miami?"

"Couldn't I be a clown again?" Jimmie asked. "I love sculpting balloons and running around in those floppy shoes with the false nose and the polka-dot jumpsuit."

"I want you to go to boarding school, Jimmie. It's what Mom would have wanted for you: a good education. We have her insurance money now, and she would want you to use it that way."

"I'm getting a good education on the Internet."

"Ms. Fondaloot told me you had some trouble at the BrainPower audition. She said you needed to hit the books more."

"You told me to count my victories, not to think about saying 'consensus of opinion.' That's all I did wrong, Daddy."

"Have you written your essay about something unique in a country? I'll bet you haven't even thought of what it will be."

"It will be the Great Wall of China," said Jimmie. "It took ten years and one million people to build it."

"Okay. That's good."

"I'm going to write about it as soon as New Year's is over."

"Okay. But in Florida I'm going to get a regular job. You can't be all by yourself every day."

"I'll have Placido."

"I told you that we have to talk about that cat."

"He likes me, Dad. At night he curls up on my bed and purrs."

"Honey, I think he should probably go back where he came from."

"I was just getting used to him."

"That's why I think he should go back right away. It'll be harder the longer you wait."

"I've gotten to like him."

"He's all right for a cat, but we have to be realistic."

"Whenever you said that to Mama, remember what she always said? She always said, 'Why?'"

Sam Twilight smiled. "Yes. That was what she always said. But I don't have her to help me make decisions anymore. I just remember that she always spoke of how hard it was to be from the circus around civilians."

"She always called them lot lice, Daddy! She hated the way they looked down on her because she didn't have a good education."

"Right you are. She didn't want *you* to go through that."

"But why do I have to give up Placido?"

"What will we do with him when you go to boarding school?"

"Who said I was going to boarding school? That's not definite! Why are you telling me these bad things right before I have an audition?"

"Honey, face facts. Your last audition was for the part of a cookie crumb, and now Fiona wants you to try out for face in the crowd. You're not going *up*hill."

"I don't want Placido to go back to Critters!"

"When I got him for you, I was remembering how much Mom liked Siamese. And I was sure you'd land BrainPower and we'd stay up north. But now I have to rethink everything."

Placido decided to jump down to the sun spot and roll over in an adorable pose, paws out, whiskers brisk, tail still, eye rolled back.

"Look, Dad."

"I see him. But every time I put Dancer's picture back, he swats it down the crack where your frog landed, minus its tongue. Placido doesn't come when he's called. He doesn't eat until he feels like it. He's never around to greet us when we come back here. For Christmas I paid six ninety-eight for the CatnipJumper at Pets Galore and he didn't even look at it. What about the catnip mouse you bought him? He smelled it once. Period."

It had no smell was why. The catnip in those toys

was probably put there way back in the year I was with my first owner (whom I never discuss), thought Placido.

"Daddy? There's the limo. Just promise you haven't made up your mind yet about any of this."

"We'll see," said Sam Twilight.

Placido jumped to his feet and headed under the table. He was despondent as he thought, We all know what "we'll see" means. We all know what a sneaky reply "we'll see" is.

25

To Dream
the Impossible Dream

oof! Woof! Woof! Woof! How could one endure the endless barking coming from the pig-faced Posh?

Marshall slithered over to his water bowl and wound himself around it into a neat little coil of king snake. Walter had brought him another live rat, sat with him while he got it down, and told him that soon he would be going to New York City to live with his father. It would be dreadful to lose Walter, for not only was he a dear friend, but also Walter knew more about snakes than anyone at Critters did. He knew, for instance, that Marshall was a very good swimmer and that even water snakes feared him, for if he was hungry, he went right in after one.

Despite the fact that Marshall was a pragmatic realist, very occasionally he allowed himself to daydream. It was the same dream over and over, delightful and impossible, a dream of a young, knowledgeable boy coming to Critters to adopt him. As the new year was about to begin, Marshall added a flourish or two. The boy would be Walter. Walter had prepared a vivarium where he lived with his father at Ritzy Riverview Apartments. He was at Critters to collect Marshall and take him to live there, in the company of exotic plants and soft green moss, with a real stream winding through it.

Of course it would never happen. That's why it was an impossible dream.

That New Year's Eve afternoon, many of the dogs at Critters had impossible dreams. The rumor had spread that Flo Tintree was on her way. One of them would spend the holiday at the Star-Tintrees', along with Catherine, whose stay had been extended. Mrs. Tintree would select one animal, which she would write a skit about, or a song, or something to amuse and teach the children. It was a tradition.

Who didn't dare hope that he would be the chosen one?

Marshall, for one. An impossible dream was different from hope, for it was understood that it was just a dream. . . . But hope was the worst of all evils, for it only prolonged misery.

Everyone was edgy anyway. Holidays did that. Volunteers were busy with their families and sometimes did not show up to walk the dogs.

Visitors were few.

Outside, the winter wind howled.

The critters slept too much and waited, as they always waited, for their fates to change.

Marshall felt the only thing that could change in his life was the lightbulb directly over his cage. It was changed when it went out. Marshall was the only critter to have one, for it was necessary to keep him warm. A cold snake became sluggish and refused to eat.

If Catherine had still been there, Marshall would have bet her that Mrs. Tintree was coming for Posh. As much as Catherine liked to bet, she probably wouldn't have taken him up on that one.

Not only was Posh the most valuable and rare dog in residence, Posh never stopped barking. Wasn't there an old saying about the squeaky wheel getting the grease?

26

A Mystery Guest

atherine's treatment in the Star-Tintree house had undergone a radical change ever since she had rescued Peke from the scowling chauffeur of the long white limousine.

"Come and play with me, Catherine," said Peke, who could not get enough of Catherine now. After all, she was his savior.

"I am played out, Peke. I am not used to running around anymore. My hind legs give."

Catherine was stretched out on the old thick carpet by the fireplace while Peke stood over her with a chew stick in his mouth.

Flo Tintree was testing the floorboards of the small stage she had built. She said, "When our mystery guest comes tomorrow night, you'll have to give up your place by the fire, Catherine. I know you're never warm enough, but the mystery guest does not even have hair." She was fixing the stage for her performance.

Peke dropped the chew stick so he could ask Catherine, "Do *you* know who's coming here?"

"I overheard Ginny tell Nell there's a new kind of Mexican hairless dog at Critters now. It's called a fancy long name, xoloitzcuintle. Xolo for short."

"Bolo, solo, polo—yes, there are words to rhyme xolo with. Mrs. Tintree will compose a good song."

"Why does she bring an animal here just for the New Year's party?" Catherine asked.

"Because," said Peke, "she's a retired school-teacher. It's her nature to teach. She likes Sun Lily's school friends to learn about animals. I don't know why she can't invite a more presentable critter. Why do we have to have one with no hair? Why not a soft little bunny?"

"Even if Critters did have bunnies, which they don't, I would have to chase a soft little bunny," said Catherine. "That is my nature, just as teaching is Mrs. Tintree's."

"Then I would help you," said Peke, who would do almost anything for the greyhound now.

He had already shown Catherine his hiding place, and even though Catherine had lost the bet that she could find it on her own, Peke had given her his red rubber hot dog.

Catherine had to pretend that she was overwhelmed by the gift of the red rubber hot dog, but the truth was she was *under*whelmed by anything she had not won in a bet.

Mrs. Tintree said, "Maybe before I start dinner, I should try out my new song on you. Would you like that?"

Peke barked, and so did Catherine.

She took a slip of paper from the pocket of her sweater and began to sing in a shaky soprano voice.

> "I'm partial to Marshall, the one of whom I sing.
> Black with yellow crossbands, he is a real king!
> See him on his tree branch, looped around and round,
> See him flick his tongue, silently, no sound!
> Mice are nice for Marshall's feasts,
> He will eat all sorts of beasts.
> He can even happily make
> Dinner of another snake.
> Marshall, I am partial to you.
> Marshall, we all say 'howdy do'!"

Peke's little eyes were wide with astonishment.

"A snake!" he cried out. "The most loathsome of all beasts!"

"Marshall?" Catherine could still not believe it. *Marshall?*

27

Goldie?

Sam ("We'll See") Twilight was careless with his tools.

There they were, out on the aft deck where he had left them in the middle of repairing the rotting wood.

And there, too, was Snack!

His pink legs were perched on the man's saw. He had a clam in his yellow bill, which he was throwing to the deck. Once, twice, until he finally broke the shell. Then he gobbled down the insides.

Placido's jaws trembled with excitement. His whole body quivered. His ruff was up.

If wishes could break glass, that gull would be a goner in a nanosecond.

Placido watched him take off, swoop, and sail as he flapped his gray wings. And then . . . and then . . . what did Placido see?

He crouched down and fixed his eye on a dog heading toward a boat on the next dock.

Placido knew that dog!

He was on a leash, heeling, while a lady shuffled along toward the big fishing boat called *We All Make Mistakes*.

"Goldie!" Placido stood up on his hind legs with his paws against the glass.

Then he tried "Rex!"

But there was no way the dog could see Placido, much less hear him.

Had Goldie found his owner? Could that be Bob's mother?

28
The Stray

"How are you, Serefina?" the fisherman said. "Come on in. Who's this? Why, he looks just like Elio."

The woman led Goldie inside. "He's not Elio, though," she said. "He'll never be Elio either. I call him Elio, but that's where the similarity ends."

The fisherman patted Goldie's head. "He's a nice dog, though."

Goldie wagged his tail and tried to smile.

He could smell coffee. Then he sniffed the man's pant leg, and it smelled of the sea, the way the beaches he had run along with Bob smelled.

"Where'd you get him, Serefina?"

"He's just a stray."

"The good Lord provides. Elio died and now you

have another almost like him."

"He's not at all like him." The woman took her coat off. She said, "He can't sing."

The fisherman chuckled. "Well, Elio was unusual."

"I'll say he was. This dog has no fun in him!"

"Give him time."

"I will, but it's hard. Elio understood everything I said, even when I said it in Spanish. I loved that dog like I'd love a son. He was almost human."

Goldie sat down and sighed. He knew how the woman felt, because Bob felt that way about him. He could only imagine what Bob must be going through now. He couldn't stop thinking about Bob, remembering his smile, his voice saying, "Rex? Want to go for a walk?"

"Is that Elio's collar and tags he's wearing?" the fisherman asked.

"Yes. I don't want him to run away."

The fisherman was pouring coffee. He said, "Maybe it would be a good idea to call this dog by another name. You can't replace Elio. Give this guy a different identity."

"What shall I call him?" she asked.

"Name him after me, Serefina. Call him Bob!"

Goldie began to bark at Bob's name.

"He seems to like the idea," said Serefina.

"Do you want to be called Bob?" the fisherman asked Goldie.

Goldie barked and barked.

"Bob it is!" said Serefina. "Okay. Bob! You're named Bob!"

Goldie got up on his hind legs, barking and barking, his paws on the counter, the coffee cup tipping over.

Serefina jumped back.

The fisherman took away the cup and mopped up the coffee.

"He couldn't help that," said the fisherman.

"Remember how graceful Elio was? He didn't have a wrong move in him," said Serefina.

Goldie crouched down, his tail between his legs.

"I may have an answer to this, Serefina," said the fisherman. "There is a rather shabby, somewhat ailing woman who is looking for a dog. I didn't pay much attention to what she said, but she left a phone number. Shall I see if this fellow here is hers?"

"Even if he isn't hers," Serefina said, "see if she wants him."

29

"The Dragon Is Dancing"

The talent, of course, does not mingle with the audience before the performance.

That was always the rule.

"But not tonight," Sam Twilight said. "One of the reasons I took this job was so you could meet some kids your own age. I'll give you plenty of time to change before our act."

"Okay," said Jimmie. She actually felt good. She had slept aboard *Summer Salt II* with Placido curled up beside her. She had told him her woes, and he had licked away her tears with his sandpaper tongue.

She had told him about being too dumb for the BrainPower commercial, too wide-eyed for the part of crumb, and then the lowest blow of all, too ordinary for face in the crowd.

If that wasn't bad enough, Ms. Fondaloot had left her with a cleaning bill for hairs on the brown crumb costume and upchuck and hairs on her black cashmere DKNY coat.

"When you tell your father about all of this, don't blame me," she'd said. "None of this was my doing."

Of course it wasn't Fiona Fondaloot's doing. None of anything that went bad was an agent's doing; an agent's doing was a callback, a sale, a contract, residuals.

Jimmie didn't tell her father anything, and he was at the point now where he didn't ask how an audition went. She was glad she didn't have to admit that she wasn't even able to get the part of face in the crowd. She had met a girl her age weeping in the john because she had not qualified for back of the head in the same crowd.

"Hey, Jimmie? Come and meet my friends!" Sun Lily was coming toward her.

Treat it like a gig, Jimmie told herself, not like a party.

But she had no lines. She couldn't say, "A yogin is one who practices mental training or discipline." She couldn't say, "Where did the little crumb come from? Not from a Ballbat cookie."

Then Sun Lily was grinning at her, holding out the Walkman, saying, "I love 'The Dragon Is Dancing'!"

"You like his music?" said Jimmie.

"We all do. I played the CD for my friends, too!"

The Pekingese and the greyhound trotted after them.

"I can tell you I am fed up with that song," Peke complained. "Do we have to hear it day and night?"

"I don't mind it," Catherine said.

"You don't mind anything, Catherine. A snake is in the house and you have no reaction. That race-track damaged you dreadfully, dear."

"Be nice to Marshall, Peke. He never gets asked anywhere."

"Oh, what a surprise *that* is," said Peke.

"He is a very smart snake. He taught me the word 'depauperate.' I bet you don't know what it means. Want to bet?"

"Why should I know what it means? I don't talk snake."

"It means 'stunted or severely diminished.'"

Peke wrinkled up his nose and shrugged. "Why would anyone say 'depauperate' when 'stunted or severely diminished' means the same thing?"

"Because, Peke, it's good to have a big vocabulary."

"You will do anything to be liked, Catherine," Peke said. "Your heritage, as you presume to call it, has taken its toll. Mine has made me particular. You might even say that I am a wee bit snobbish, since I am descended from Lootie, who was Queen Victoria's dog."

"So you keep telling everyone, Peke. But I thought you were from China, the same as Sun Lily."

"No, my ancestors were. Then when the British sacked Peking (from whence came our name), they chose us as a gift fit for the queen," said Peke with another smug sniff of his nose. "And others of my ancient Asian ancestors were palace pooches who hung out with the emperor."

"You think too much about how aristocratic your ancestors were," said Catherine.

"You *never* can think too much about that, Catherine. . . . But I do not find you a depauperate companion," Peke answered, his mouth curling up with pleasure at his own cleverness.

"C'mon, Catherine and Peke. Keep up with us," Sun Lily called out. "Walter Splinter is here too," she told Jimmie Twilight. "You know him, don't you?"

"The boy from Critters?"

"And guess what! His father is here. His father is

famous. We heard his father broadcast from Israel just the other night, and now he's in our house. Turn right, Jimmie. We're going down the back way."

"Where to?"

"The basement. My grandmother is going to put on a little show. She does it every year."

"What kind of a show?" They were heading down the stairs.

"It's always different."

"Oh, this one's going to be different, that's for sure," Peke muttered to Catherine.

Sam Twilight appeared behind them on the stairs, heading for Mrs. Tintree's performance himself.

Sun Lily looked over her shoulder at Jimmie and said, "What about Jimmie Spheeris? Was he as famous as Walter's father?"

"Was he, Dad?"

"No, Spheeris wasn't that well-known. Now he's sort of a cult personality."

"Like Elvis Presley?" Sun Lily asked.

"He was never that big. But you can find him on the Internet. There's a web page for him, even though he's dead."

"Guess what, Jimmie."

"What?"

Whatever Sun Lily said, Jimmie couldn't hear it,

for when she opened the door at the bottom of the stairs, the noise of the party drowned out her words. Sun Lily ran ahead of her.

When Jimmie looked down, a thin length of something that looked like a hose with eyes peered back at her, a tongue darting out, flicking.

Then "Eeeeeeeeeeek!" Jimmie cried out. "A snake!"

Sun Lily was cupping her mouth with her hand, laughing, saying, "I just tried to tell you to watch out, there'd be a snake."

Jimmie jumped away from the stairs while the dogs ran past her, barking.

"A snake!" Her heart was pounding.

"He's big, too," said Sam Twilight.

Sun Lily said, "He's a king, but Grandmother says he's not a king of any country. He's just a king!"

30

"The One of Whom I Sing"

> "He can even happily make
> Dinner of another snake."

But Marshall had dropped down into his wood chips, and stayed there, soon after the girl had screamed "Eeeeeeeeeeek! A snake!"

> "Marshall, I am partial to you.
> Marshall, we all say 'howdy do'!"

Applause.

Applause, even though no one could see Marshall. Only a few very watchful members of the audience had seen him at all.

"Oh, dear, dear, dear," Mrs. Tintree exclaimed. "I think all this fuss over him has frightened him, but he's there. You can just about see his yellow cross-bands."

Then, buried in the wood chips, Marshall heard a familiar sound.

It was Catherine barking at his cage. "She went all the way to Critters for you, Marshall. The least you can do is show yourself."

"Want to bet I won't?" Marshall answered her.

"Please get the dogs away from his cage!" Mrs. Tintree called out. "I believe he is frightened of the dogs."

Then, miraculously, Marshall felt warm fingers reach for him, and he heard Walter say, "Would you like to meet my dad, Marshall?"

All the screams, crude remarks, and unpleasant noises a snake had to endure when he appeared in public filled the recreation room of the Star-Tintree house. But Walter's loving hands were warm and sure.

31
The Gig

They used a downstairs guest room to get into their costumes.

Sam Twilight was wearing a sheet around him, and he would carry the scythe that was resting against the wall. In the circus he had often been the clown chased by the skeleton. On his face was a mask frozen into a look of horror. A papier-mâché skeleton was fastened to the back of his wide red-silk trousers. The polka-dot arms of his costume flapped as he raced ahead, looking over his shoulder, only to find the deathly figure still in pursuit of him. Kids loved that act.

Jimmie had changed to her Twinkle Toes tutu and was lacing up her dance shoes.

"How do you like these young people, Jimmie?"

"The only one I've really had a chance to talk with is Sun Lily."

"And?"

"And she's fine, Dad. Stop worrying about me."

He walked over to the bed and sat down, shaking his head. "I could see your mother in you tonight."

"Thanks."

"It's not really a compliment, Jimmie." He cleared his throat the way he always did before he said something he didn't enjoy saying. "I see now that we really do have to sell *Summer Salt II*."

"You love that boat."

"I love you more, Jimmie. I've got to get you into a good school. You're going to miss out on your teen years if I don't. I want you to have normal teenage years."

"Why? So I can hang out with kids who all dress alike? They all have on the same kind of clothes. Ralph Lauren, Tommy Hilfiger, Armani. Do you want me to be a carbon copy?" She was exaggerating, of course, and what truth there was to it hadn't bothered her at all. She imagined it was something like belonging to a club. In fact, the time at the Star-Tintrees' was passing quickly, and Jimmie was easy with everybody. But she knew her father was about to try and sell boarding school again.

"You sounded just like your mom tonight: Jimmie Spheeris, Jimmie Spheeris, Jimmy Spheeris."

Jimmie laughed. "*I* didn't start it."

"That little girl never heard of Spheeris before tonight."

"Actually, she did," Jimmie told him. "She heard of him when I dropped off the Magic House, on my way into the Ballbat audition. I lent her my CD of 'The Dragon Is Dancing.'"

"You have lots of CDs. You had to lend her one by Spheeris?"

"I always listen to him before an audition, for luck."

"*Luck?*" her father said. "Is that what you call it?"

From the other room they could hear the beginning of the countdown.

At five, the scythe went over Sam Twilight's shoulder, and Jimmie stuck the Velcro banner across her body, announcing the new year.

They went into the Magic House through a tunnel of blankets.

"I'm old and I'm weary and my job is now done." Sam Twilight was shuffling away from the Magic House wrapped in a sheet, carrying the scythe.

"There's a new year that's coming—stay well and have fun!"

Then Twinkle Toes danced out of the Magic House in her white spangled tutu, a white net sequined skirt over it, a glittering crown on her head.

"Miss New Year brings doves of peace!"

She was twisting a balloon to make a white dove.

"May all your pains and troubles cease!"

She tossed up the dove and someone caught it. She began another, saying, "'Auld Lang Syne' now shall we sing! Ring it out and ring it in!"

Then everyone began to sing while Twinkle Toes made more dove balloons.

Although she had played to larger rooms and livelier audiences, her heart was thumping with the pleasure of performing.

She could see Walter with the snake wrapped around his neck, standing beside his father. She could see Sun Lily with her school friends all grinning at her and clapping. There was Mrs. Tintree. Ginny. Nell. Mrs. Splinter. Mr. Larissa.

She sailed by them on her toe taps, while she made more white doves from her balloons.

Dotty D, the dog-faced woman, had taught Jimmie how to sculpt balloons at lunches in the pie car. It became an art with Dotty; she could make a balloon into anything: an angel, a duck, a swan, a rooster. Now so could Jimmie.

Someone had let the Pekingese and the grey-hound back into the room, and they were running after the balloons.

Dancer used to do that too. That was what dogs did. But Jimmie was thinking of Placido. She was saving one white balloon to take home. It would not be turned into a dove either. It would not be pushed playfully by black dog noses or barked at. Jimmie knew exactly what would happen to it when she blew it up and presented it to Placido.

32

33

We All Make Mist

Because her brother would not buy her eyeglasses, Ursula Uttergore had to be very close to things to understand what her eyes weren't seeing clearly.

She spoke the letters aloud. "W. e. a. l. l. m. a. k. e. m. i. s. t."

"Madam?" a voice called from the deck of the large boat. "Is that you, Madame U?"

"Yes! I am Madame U." True to her brother's rules, she never told anyone her last name, for Percival Uttergore was too well-known—and, as he enjoyed adding, too well liked—to be doing the things he forced his ailing older sister to do.

"I think you came here about the dog," the fisherman said.

"The boat I have been sent to is not called *We All Make Mist*, though that is quite a poetic name for a lobster boat, quite a poetic thought."

"*We All Make Mistakes* is her name, ma'am!"

"Yes, yes, we do," said Ursula Uttergore, whose biggest mistake in life had been answering the fatal postcard ten years past, imploring her to come "just for the summer" to care for poor young Percival, suffering from gout and greed.

"Come aboard, Madame U. I'm Robert Ketchum."

She slowly huffed and puffed her way up the gangplank.

"He's a beautiful dog," said the fisherman. He opened the small cabin door for Ursula Uttergore.

She could *see* that he was a beautiful dog. Splendid, he was!

But Ursula Uttergore had not spent a decade with Percival Uttergore and learned nothing.

She said, "He looks a bit downtrodden, captain. Did you say you were selling him?"

"No, no. I'm trying to find his owner, or at least to find someone who will give him a good home. Do you have a good home for him?"

"Does he come with bedding, with dog food, with combs, brushes, all that a dog requires?"

"I see," said the captain. "I see. He's going to

be an expense for you."

"Oh, no, no, no. I am willing to undertake the obligation. I am happy to. I was just asking routinely. Just wondering routinely."

"I do believe we can put a little money into the kitty (ha ha ha ha) toward all those things you mentioned." The fisherman reached into his back pocket for his wallet.

"Does he have a name?" she asked. She was quite sure, oh, more than quite sure, what this dog's name was, but go slowly, she told herself. She wanted her ploy to work. It was, after all, her specialty: to get a little money for herself.

"I named this fine animal after me. Bob." *Thump thump thump* went the dog's tail.

"He seems to like that name," said Ursula Uttergore, who knew he would like the name Rex even better. But no point in getting the dog excited and unable to be controlled.

The fisherman put three twenty-dollar bills on the table and said, "This is to pay some of your expenses, Madame U."

"Thank you, kind sir." One percent of whatever Rex netted (from his owner? from the medical laboratory?) plus this delightful surprise: sixty dollars.

Behind a framed travel magazine cutout of the

Eiffel Tower, Ursula kept her stash. For she was planning an escape.

To where?

She could hear the family's most wretched disappointment deriding her, saying, "I would send you away, but away to *where*, worthless, old, ailing sister? To where?"

Paris, dear failure!

Paris, unsuccessful sibling!

Paris, Percival, far from you and your furnace room and your frugal bent. I dream of Paris.

"Well, Bob," said the fisherman to the dog. "What do you think?"

Goldie looked up at Mr. Ketchum from his paws.

He wished he could say, "Can't you keep me until the real Bob finds me? I know he's looking for me. He has to be!"

"Bob wants to come home with me," Ursula Uttergore crooned in a saccharine tone Goldie sensed was shallow. "Ready, Bob? Ready?"

No.

Not ready.

34

A Snake Is a Snake
Is a Snake

Even though a snake is accustomed to sensing pejorative remarks about his appearance, his movements, and his eating habits, do not believe for one minute that it is okay with him. In truth, it affects his self-esteem dreadfully.

When it happens on the first day of the new year, a snake wonders just how he is expected to slither through three hundred sixty-four more days.

"—not my idea of a pet!" the world-famous globe-trotter said in his deep and important CNN voice.

Marshall slid down the neck of Walter's shirt and lumped himself inside, feeling the boy's warm skin.

"But you said I could have any kind of pet I wanted," Walter complained.

"I doubt very, very much that they even allow snakes at Ritzy Riverview Apartments, son. Snakes are slimy."

"Feel, Daddy. Put your hand inside my shirt. He's not slimy."

"I just had a manicure, Walter. I have to do World Roundup tonight."

Over by the fireplace, Catherine and Peke lay huddled together, listening.

Guy Splinter said, "Of all the pets in the world you could have, why would you choose one who's always sticking his tongue out at you?"

"Good point!" Peke said.

"Dad, that's how Marshall investigates his surroundings."

"Want to bet Walter ends up adopting Posh and not Marshall?" Catherine asked Peke.

"You have nothing to bet, Catherine."

"Just bet. You don't need anything to just bet. I bet this famous newsman will want an unusual pet so people will say he's unusual too."

"He's already unusual, Catherine. You said yourself he's famous."

Guy Splinter said, "Marshall has no eyelids. His eyes look ominous staring at you."

"He smells, too," Catherine told Peke.

"He *smells?*" Peke said.

"I never smelled him, but it's rumored that when he's very afraid, he smells."

"Look over there by the fireplace, son," said the world-famous globe-trotter who broadcast from anyplace but where his family was. "See *them?* They are my idea of pets. . . . I can understand why Ginny and Nell are adopting the greyhound. If I had a dog that sleek and loving, I wouldn't take it back to Critters either."

Catherine stood up. "Peke? Peke? Did you hear that? I'm being adopted." Catherine was just about to bark blissfully.

"Hush, Catherine!" Peke commanded. "Don't bark! I want to hear the rest of this. I knew you were being adopted last night."

"And you didn't tell me?"

"Purposely."

"But why, Peke?"

"You have a lot to learn about canine psychology, Catherine."

"I thought you liked me."

"Enormously, yes. But I will not be top dog anymore. That makes me quite sad, Catherine. You wouldn't understand because you have never been top dog."

"But Peke, I—"

"Shhh. Hush, please. I want to see if Walter can convince his father to accept a snake."

"I'll bet he can't," said Catherine. "Want to bet, Peke?"

"No, Catherine. And now that you are joining the Star-Tintree family, you had better shape up. We are not a dissolute family like some. There is no alcoholism, no one smokes, no one watches daytime TV, and, my dear new sister, *no one* gambles!"

"I still bet Walter won't get his father to adopt Marshall."

"Children manipulate parents, Catherine. I've seen it time and time again."

"Not Walter or Sun Lily, though."

"Oh, Catherine, you are so naive. It's a good thing you're joining the family. You wouldn't last a day in the cruel world outside these walls."

Walter was saying to his father, "Maybe if *you* won't let me have Marshall, Mother *will*. Maybe I should live with Mother in New Jersey."

"Now it begins," Peke said.

35

Belonging

"'The last time I saw Paris,'" sang Ursula Uttergore, who had never seen the French capital. "Yes, my dear dog, you are in good hands now. We are walking the gangplank! Heel, dear, heel, oh, my, you mind very nicely."

Goldie knew he was very far from Critters, because there was no water near any of the paths the volunteers walked dogs down.

He might have tried to break away and run, for he could tell the woman leading him could probably not hold him.

But what good would running do, even if he had the strength left to do it?

The fisherman had not fed him, only put down a

bowl of water for him. He had not had very much to eat for a day and a night. He believed this woman would give him a meal, and a place to sleep, for she did not appear to be a cruel woman. She seemed to want him badly. Would he have to accept the idea that he had lost both his home and his friends at Critters, and now he should take whatever he could find for a home?

At least he was safe from the dogcatcher, for if he stayed with this woman, he would belong to someone.

The woman continued singing about Paris, walking with Goldie by the water, the brown Bronco following at a safe distance.

36

That Could Be Me!

nyone could tell you that the brains behind
BrainPower were not the brains of Quintin
Quick. They were the brains of his wife, Myrna
Quick, B.S., M.A., Ph.D., and founder of W.O.E.,
Wives of Executives.

New Year's Day found them breakfasting in their
luxurious suite at the Waldorf-Astoria.

"Remember the young fellow you called loopy?"
she said as she dug into her eggs Benedict. "What
was his name?"

"Cane. Cole Cane. Loopy looking. I used my
memory trick on that boy. Trouble. Raise Cain. A
soul as black as coal. Cole Cane."

"And what is the name of the model you finally
hired?"

"Oh, I'd have to look that up. He had a very high I.Q. Perfect for the part of Art Smart.

"Fire him," said Myrna Quick. "Get Cane."

"Ha ha, that's a good one," said her husband, who didn't think it was that good a joke, but who knew it was wise to humor his beloved.

"I'm serious, Quintin! You can remember Cole Cane, but you can't remember the one you hired. Do you think the televiewing and Internet audience is going to remember him?"

"Well, I—"

"Hire the loopy one! Pass the salt, please. I even like his name: Cole Cane. We don't want a real brain to represent us. A real brain, Quintin, has no use for us. We're selling Brainstorm."

"Oh, my, oh, my. Why didn't I think of that?"

"Because you don't have to. You have me. Next, Jane Brain. It's all right to call her that for now, but we'll probably use her real name. She could have a room-temperature I.Q. and it wouldn't matter for now. We want someone with potential. Pretty, personable, young, and not the smug type who isn't capable of mispronunciation, misspelling, and making mistakes!"

"I see your point, Myrna," said Quintin Quick.

"We want our audience to sympathize with her."

"Quite true," said Quintin.

"To identify with her!"

"Quite true," said Quintin.

"We want to educate her in full view of everyone!"

"Is that what we want?"

"And everyone will think: That could be me. . . . Not a bad title for the Brainstorm television segments. That could be me."

"That could be me," Quintin Quick murmured, munching on his caviar popover, swallowing his coffee, remembering someone suddenly.

"Who *did* you hire for Jane Brain?" his wife asked as she buttered her toast and watched out of the corner of her eye *The Bag and Shoe Shopper* on channel 345.

"No one yet, dearest, but I'm going to take care of that now. Hand me the phone, please."

"Who are you calling on New Year's Day?"

"Fiona Fondaloot," her husband answered, looking for the name on his speed dial.

"We'll see Jane Brain through high school, college—we'll go the limit with her," said Myrna Quick. "With some tutors, and a good private school, she'll be living proof that Brainstorm works!"

"Ms. Fondaloot?" her husband said into the telephone. "I'm sorry to bother you on New Year's Day.

But we at BrainPower want very much to reach Consensus of Opinion."

"Quin-tin," Myrna Quick whispered with a frown across her forehead. "*What* are you saying? Consensus *means* opinion!"

"That's right, Ms. Fondaloot," said her husband. "You remember her. She spoke out of turn."

37

A Flying Lesson

P O P! And it had been the start of a new year.

Placido had seen it in grandly, drunk on high-quality catnip Jimmie had given him after he broke the balloon with one sure bite.

Then Placido had rolled around the floor of the galley, run madly through the cabins, nudged Dancer's picture back down the crack beside the tongueless Roscoe the Robotic Frog, gobbled up a bit of Friskies sliced beef in gravy, urped, and chased his tail madly as Jimmie hollered, "Oh, no, Pla-ci-do!"

But Jimmie was laughing, for she had begun to appreciate the true Placido: playful, distinguished with his one blue eye, superior, as all Siamese are, and deserving of adoration. Placido fell into a tipsy sleep knowing that he adored her, too.

When he woke up on New Year's Day, he strolled around groggily for a while, until he jumped up on her bunk and enjoyed an early-morning siesta curled beside her pillow.

His new life aboard *Summer Salt II* was turning out satisfactorily. He had never believed it could, after living with his first owner (whom he never discussed), but what was he if he wasn't happy?

He got up when Jimmie and her father did, accepted a few pieces of bacon from their breakfasts, cleaned his paws atop the small refrigerator, and tried to decide which one to hang out with.

It should be Sam Twilight, he knew. He had yet to win *him* over. He hadn't dared perch near him and purr, for fear he would be thrust to the cabin floor. You could never gauge a male's reaction to soft, seductive moves. Placido would have to plan his approach carefully, do a few darling things first like drape himself across a bureau top, hang a paw down, fling a leg back, look at the gentleman with eyes half closed, *purrrrrr*.

As it turned out, there was no way he could hang out with Sam Twilight. The man still had carpentry left to do on the aft deck.

Placido hopped across to Jimmie's desk, where she

sat doing her homework on the computer. He liked to see the strange shapes she brought up on the screen. He liked to purr and have her see him near, reach out, and tickle him under his chin. What was that if it wasn't bonding? Big time!

But Jimmie answered the phone after about half an hour, said a few words, listened, then jumped up and called to Twilight: "Daddy! Daddy! Come inside, Daddy! Good news!"

When Sam Twilight came in from the deck, Jimmie said, "Ms. Fondaloot says Mr. Quick wants to see me."

"What for?"

"She said Mr. Quick called her, and he wanted the girl who said 'consensus of opinion.'"

"*What?*"

"That's what Ms. Fondaloot said, Daddy!"

"Oh, honey, Jimmie, that doesn't sound right. There's something fishy here, sweetheart."

"I can only tell you what Ms. Fondaloot said. I'm supposed to go into New York tomorrow morning."

"Are you sure you heard her right?" Sam Twilight shook his head.

"I heard her right. She's surprised too."

"Don't get your hopes up, honey."

"I know. . . . But if I got work in New York City,

we could live out here on *Summer Salt II* and we could keep Placido."

"It sounds too good to be true," Sam Twilight said.

Jimmie put her arms around him, and they hugged.

Placido reacted to this glimmer of good news the same way Sam Twilight had—suspiciously. Then he felt an enormous fatigue overcome him, his usual response to doubt, dread, and fear.

He padded away, down the hall toward the master's cabin. It was time for his second nap of the day, which meant he had nineteen naps to go. Better get started, Sailor, he said to himself, for that was the name he had decided to take if this was to be his permanent home. A cat on a boat was not your average cat. A cat on a boat should have a nautical name.

Up on the shelf in the sun spot for nap number two.

But whoa, wait a minute, wait . . . a . . . minute.

Placido, aka Sailor, surveyed the scene before him.

Puffy white clouds above, rippling blue water below, and there on the aft deck, sitting on the saw left there by Sam Twilight, was Snack!

The gull was swallowing down something dead from the water.

Sailor felt his teeth chatter and his jaws tremble. And he felt something else. Something very slight, but very plainly fresh air. Something that was not blowing in through a crack either.

And then Sailor Placido saw it.

Sam Twilight must have opened it as he was working out there.

Sailor Placido moved down the shelf in a crouch toward the porthole.

He nudged it with his head. His whiskers felt the wind, then his nose did, then his ears.

He could just about squeeze through.

The stupid, garbage-mouth gull just sat there on his pink legs, the tail of some old fish disappearing inside him.

Placido's one eye was open wide with joy and disbelief as he targeted his prey.

One quick leap would do it.

Placido's behind shook in preparation.

His back legs flexed for the jump.

ONE . . . TWO . . . and on THREE, Placido the Sailor became Placido the Flyer, sailing out into the morning wind, just as Snack, too, took off.

The difference was that Snack could fly.

Placido's target disappeared while his flight continued.

Out, out, then down, down.

SPLASH!

Placido sank into the bay, emerging with flailing paws.

Wet, wretched paws that were searching for something to grip.

But to grip with *what*?

Not with his claws, for he had none.

38
Help!

Going down for the third time, Placido thought of how the animals at Critters always called out, "Good-bye, Placido!"

Now there was no one to wish him farewell.

Off in the distance there was the sound of a boat's horn, a dog barking, and the wind blowing the waves into whitecaps.

It was very likely Placido would drown here in Gardiner's Bay, and as terrified as he was at the prospect, he was also appalled to realize that his body could float in the bay for days on end. Who would know where his poor body was?

It was quite possible that a fourteen-pound, one-eyed sealpoint Siamese would turn into fish fodder, and then Placido had another thought as he gagged on the salty bay water. It was quite possibly his last thought.

HE COULD BECOME A SNACK FOR SNACK!

What a degrading payback for all the mean, urpy, crabby, crappy, bullying, boisterous feline pranks he had committed in his tempestuous time on earth!

What a cruel twist of fate, just as he had his sea legs, his sailor identity, and for now, anyway, a new seafaring family.

So this was the end of him, was it?

Good-bye, Placido.

So long, Sailor.

And then and there, Placido died.

Died . . . and to his great surprise went to heaven.

For what would you call it when you saw the great golden light at the end of the tunnel?

What could that grip on your neck be but the angel pulling you out of the water, carrying you aloft, seeing you to shore?

If this was not your guardian angel helping you to ascend to the clouds above, what would you call it?

"Luck," said Goldie. "Boy, are you ever in luck, Placido!"

Chilled to the bone, not dead at all, not even

close to heaven, Placido lay on the ground beside the pier, panting for breath.

"How did *you* get here, Goldie?"

"I had just come down the gangplank of *We All Make Mistakes*, walking along with this woman, when I heard a voice cry, 'Sister! Ursula!' from a dirty brown Bronco. I knew that car, and I knew who those red gloves on the wheel belonged to. The dog-catcher! Uttergore! Then I saw your splash, and I broke free of Madame U, and I swam as fast as I could away from them and toward you. . . . Let me get my breath."

"You swam to rescue *me?*"

"I did not know it was you, Placido. I have to be honest."

"Then why did you swim after me?"

"It's in my nature. I am not a Labrador retriever for nothing!"

Goldie had been the dog, then, standing on the pier barking, as he dove into the bay.

At least three people had witnessed his gallant rescue of Placido. Now they were running toward the pair. The fisherman, Jimmie, and Sam Twilight.

"That's the stray I just gave to Madame U!" said the fisherman. Jimmie bent down and picked Placido up, hugging him to her, even though he was soaking wet. "Oh, Placido! We almost lost you! Daddy left that porthole open."

"A stray?" Mr. Twilight said, bending over to pet Goldie. "You wouldn't be Goldie, would you? You wouldn't be Rex?"

Goldie barked and shook himself, barked and shook himself, and barked.

"Come along, Goldie, Rex, I think we know someone who's looking for you."

Placido began to purr in Jimmie's arms.

Goldie walked along with them as they headed toward *Summer Salt II*.

Down on the road a rusty brown Bronco was turning around to head the other way.

"Thanks, Goldie," said Placido. "Thanks, Rex."

"You're welcome," said Goldie. Then he saw where they were going, and he said, "A boat? You live on a boat now, Placido?"

Placido, rapturous in the arms of Jimmie Twilight, interrupted his purring long enough to answer, "Aye, aye, sir! Welcome aboard!"

39

The Perilous Present

It was the day after New Year's Day.

Walter Splinter knelt before Marshall's cage. "I tried everything to get Dad to keep you," he told the snake, who had heard him trying at the Star-Tintrees'. "He's dead set against it. He says I have to grow up and learn to care about *people*."

Not an easy task, Marshall mumbled to himself.

"I'm not going to say good-bye. It's too sad. But I'll be back to visit Grandma. I'll see you then."

Walter fled before the tears in his eyes spilled down his cheeks.

After Walter left, Irving waited for Marshall to settle down. Irving had a new little cot, with a plaid cedar cushion on it. It was a Christmas gift from

Mrs. Silverman, the volunteer who walked him every day. She had arthritis too, so she knew it would make Irving more comfortable, and still the workers would be able to wash out his cage.

"Walter hated leaving you, didn't he?" Irving finally spoke up. "He took it really hard."

Marshall had climbed up into his plastic tree to hang around. He was not keen on discussing any hard feelings of Walter Splinter.

He said, "When did Baldy go?"

"Posh went yesterday. Do you want to know something unusual? Posh needs to be smeared with sunscreen before she goes outdoors. I heard Mrs. Splinter give the new owner directions."

"I hope she croaks," said Marshall.

"Be careful or you'll develop a bitter streak," said Irving.

"Who wouldn't? Look around, Irving. First Placido went, and this time it looks like he'll have a home. I heard Mrs. Splinter say that Goldie was back home. Then the Star-Tintrees decided to keep Catherine. Then, let's see, there's Dewey—"

Irving interrupted him. "It's better not to dwell on it."

"Do you call what I'm doing over here dwelling? This is not dwelling. This is hanging here pointlessly, nothing to look forward to but a frozen mouse. You know, all the taste is gone out of them once they're defrosted."

Irving's eyes rolled away from Marshall wound around his tree branch. It was better to stay at Critters forever than to go on an overnight visit. A tiny taste of home was a real killer.

Irving knew that there was nothing he could do or say to cheer up his twisted pal, but he always made an effort.

"*Days of Our Lives* is coming on soon," he said. "They're still in the midst of that murder trial. It could be exciting, Marshall, and I'll tell you everything that's happening."

"You've settled for a life of watching soaps, Irving."

"It's not such a bad life, now that I have my plaid cedar cushion. There is plenty going on! Births and deaths, betrayals, weddings, funerals, everything in life is in that show."

"There are no snakes, however."

Irving had to agree. He had never seen a snake on a soap.

"I'm going to take a nap," Marshall said. "I'm going to try and dream something magnificent. At least all sleeping dreams are true while they last."

The sun was sinking and Mrs. Splinter was getting ready to lock up when Irving heard a voice he recognized.

"Do you remember me, Mrs. Splinter? Mom's parking the car."

"Why, Bob! Bob Randall! Goldie hasn't run away again, I hope!"

"We call him Rex. Rex is fine. Happy New Year!"

"You came all the way from Montauk to wish me a Happy New Year?"

"That's part of the reason we came," said Bob. "The other part is that I'd like to be interviewed for an adoption."

Irving lifted his head from his paws to hear better.

"Do you have a particular animal in mind?"

"Yes, ma'am. When I was here looking for Rex, I saw that beautiful king snake you have. Is he still here?"

Irving barked and jumped up and down to jolt Marshall from his sleep.

"Thanks a lot, Irving," Marshall complained. "I was just beginning to dream I was adopted."

"You're going to be, Marshall."

"I'll tell you something about yourself, Irving. You're too much of an optimist. Life is a struggle.

Why can't you acknowledge that dreams don't come true? What dream of yours has ever come true?"

"My dream of a soft bed came true," said Irving. "But this isn't about me—listen!"

Mrs. Splinter was continuing with the interview.

"Have you ever lived with a snake, Bob?"

"Never. But I'd take good care of him, ma'am. I know a lot about snakes. I've been thinking of him ever since I saw him back there. My mother said that if I was serious, she'd bring me down here so I could talk with you about it. My mother says it would be a way to repay Critters for the time you spent on Rex. And it would be my birthday present."

Irving was up on all fours, wagging his tail.

"Did you hear that, Marshall?"

Unfurled, winding himself down toward his wood chips, Marshall's tongue darted in and out so fast he could not talk.

Sometimes impossible dreams come true, even for a serpent.

40
Home

Mrs. Randall, Bob, and his baby sister were still not home when Rex tried once more to get Rags' attention.

"Just tell me if you missed me," Rex said.

"Were you gone?" Rags answered.

"Was I *gone*? I was lost for weeks! Didn't you even notice that I was gone? Why, Percival Uttergore was out looking for me wearing his red gloves! His tricky sister fetched me and was taking me to the dirty brown Bronco!"

Rags cleaned his ears with his paws.

"Was I *gone*?" Rex bellowed. "I was at Critters, and I was running through the woods! I was in a house with a piano and the lady got mad at me because I couldn't sing! I had horns honking at me, branches catching my collar and tags, and I was even on a boat! Was I *gone?*"

Rags had hind toes to clean plus nails to bite down on all four feet. He had his tail to attend to, and his belly.

"I even imagined you were calling me home. . . . And you won't believe this, Rags, but I saved a cat."

Rags yawned. Soon he would have to check out the action in the yard. He would have to chase away the unkempt Persian cat with all the mats in her hair, and he would have to climb a tree or two.

"There's this one-eyed Siamese named Placido," said Rex, but he could not finish telling Rags about him, because the door opened right at that moment.

In came Mrs. Randall, followed by Bob and his little sister.

Bob was carrying the kind of case cats come in.

"What's this?" Rags asked.

"I can't imagine," Rex answered.

Bob set the case down on the floor.

He said, "Rags and Rex, you have a new brother." He opened the top, and in a few seconds out came—

"Marshall!" Rex exclaimed. "Marshall!"

Rags took one look and made a dash for the cat door. Outside, his hair standing on end, his whiskers stiff, he went up a tree. On the highest branch he perched, collecting himself. A new brother, he thought, and he cleaned himself and cleaned himself, letting it sink in.

Was he expected to live with a snake?

Or was this some sneaky ploy of Bob's to unsettle him?

Whatever it was, Rags had no intention of showing that it mattered to him one way or another. For he was one clean, cool, green-eyed, sixteen-pound Maine coon cat. A poet at times, at other times not.

41

Zayit

"Who left it here, Mrs. Splinter?" the veterinarian asked.

"I have no idea. Someone opened the door yesterday morning, shoved the cage inside, and ran off."

"I heard the police had her for a while."

"What kind of lizard is it, doctor?"

"It's an iguana."

Exactly as I thought, Irving said to himself, for he had seen a program about lizards on the Animal Channel.

"Oh, dear. Is he all right? Is he healthy?"

"*She* is fine, Mrs. Splinter, but her color isn't good. She seems to have turned brown, a sign she is unhappy."

"I'll put her where Marshall was," Mrs. Splinter said.

"Let me do the honors," said Dr. Kamitses.

"Oh, dear, oh, dear. I hope she'll be all right."

"She's in good hands," the doctor said.

Irving's cage shook as the iguana's was set down. All three feet of her was reclining in a tank.

"I have to register her in my book," said Mrs. Splinter. "What shall I call her?"

"I heard that she was brought in to the police on Christmas Day," said the doctor. "Why not call her Noel?"

"Splendid idea," said Mrs. Splinter. "Come to my office and I'll give you a cup of coffee."

"Splendid idea," said the doctor.

It did not take long for Noel to do a little registering herself, for she had every reason to register many complaints. Her absentminded and eccentric owner, known to all the residents of a certain Central Park West apartment building as the Lizard Lady, had left her in a Long Island Railroad train. She was not discovered until the train stopped at Bridgehampton. Then she was taken to a drafty police station and stuck under the desk while a card game was in progress. Someone finally took her home, only to be told she could not stay there.

On and on her complaints were registered, until Irving finally shouted at her, "Please stop, Noel! I am the only one listening, and I can't do anything to relieve your misery."

"What a quandary to be in!" said Noel. "What is this awful place called? Jitters?"

"It may give you the jitters at first, but it's called Critters." Irving lifted up his rump from the soft cedar cushion and got off the cot. "It's not a bad place to be, Noel."

"Don't call me that," she snapped. "My real name is Zayit, which is Hebrew for olive, my normal color."

"Welcome to Critters, Zayit."

"That so-called veterinarian should have realized what a rare lizard I am. He would never have let me remain in a dog pound," said Zayit.

"It's not exactly a dog pound," said Irving.

"Whatever it is, *I* don't belong here," Zayit proclaimed.

"Of course you don't," Irving said, getting back on his cot, sinking into his cedar cushion, sighing.

For it was beginning again, wasn't it? A new critter, a new outcry, another declaration of superiority.

"You see," Zayit said, "not only am I a rare and

incredibly valuable lizard, but my owner is a reincarnation of Joan of Arc."

"Of course she is," said Irving.

"My life hasn't been easy," Zayit continued.

"Why don't you tell me all about it?" Irving said, for he might as well give her encouragement to do what she would do anyway. He did not mind listening either, for the more he heard of the other critters' misery, the more he thanked his lucky stars for his cage with the cot and the cedar pillow. It also made him forget how much he missed Marshall.

42

Good-bye, Placido

Jimmie told Placido everything, and everything, lately, was the same old thing. But Placido didn't care. Let her say it again and again.

"I'll get an education, Ms. Fondaloot said. Not only will the BrainPower tutor work with me when I'm in New York, but I'm applying to the Ross School out here. I'll be with Sun Lily and her friends!"

Next came the part where the cat was picked up, kissed on the cold, black, wet nose, told "We'll always be together, Placido!" then gently put back down.

Bliss!

Sailor Placido smiled to himself, for he was already

envisioning his future as mate on *Summer Salt II*.

While Jimmie wrote a letter, Sailor stayed beside her, wondering just how long it would take Snack to find his way back. Maybe he would not come back. Maybe he had never in all his days seen a flying cat and was now too terrified to return. . . . Never mind, there would be others like him. There were snacks all over the boat basin. Just let one fly too close to the porthole, and *whoosh! Bang!* Bite! Yum!

"Want to hear my letter, Placido?"

A question that did not need an answer, but Placido purred up at Jimmie, his eye closing with contentment as she read to him:

Dear Shirley and Check,

I didn't send out any Christmas cards this year, but I got yours and thanks. Guess what! I am the new spokesfemale for Brainstorm, a learning program that will be sold on TV and the Internet. Guess what else! I have a new Siamese cat named Placido.

Daddy and I are going to stay at the marina and live on our boat. In a minute I am going into New York City for rehearsal. I feel so lucky, but I will always miss our talks in the pie car and knowing people who know the musician I am named for. I'll miss getting up before the sun is up to go someplace new, and I'll miss you two. Love from Jimmie.

"Uh-oh! There's StarStretch, right on time!

"I have to go now.

"Don't wish me luck, because that's bad luck in show biz!

"I'll tell you all about it when I get back.

"Ms. Fondaloot says Cole Cane's going to be there, Placido!

"Don't let anything happen to you!

"Wait right here for me—I won't be long."

Then the inevitable parting words: "Good-bye, Placido."

Yes, there had been other good-byes, dozens, if you must know.

But this time Placido was not inside his faux-leopard carrying case, for it was locked away in the storage room.

Placido was not going anyplace.

He was home.

About the Author

M. E. Kerr is a winner of the American Library Association's Margaret A. Edwards Award for Lifetime Achievement, and of the 2000 ALAN award from the National Council of Teachers of English. Throughout her life her many pets have always come from dog pounds and animal shelters. One of them, E.R., named for Eleanor Roosevelt, was a one-eyed Siamese, similar to Placido of this book, and with the same dark secret.

Ms. Kerr lives in the Hamptons, on Long Island. Her website is: www.mekerr.com.